World Without Men

by
CHARLES ERIC MAINE

Martino Publishing
Mansfield Centre, CT
2012

Martino Publishing
P.O. Box 373,
Mansfield Centre, CT 06250 USA

ISBN 978-1-61427-227-4

© *2012 Martino Publishing*

Cover design by T. Matarazzo

Printed in the United States of America On 100% Acid-Free Paper

IN A WORLD OF ONE SEX, ANOTHER MEANS DISASTER!

Aubretia was a solid citizen of five thousand years from now. She looked upon herself as happy, normal, with the proper emotional interests, and well-adjusted to her work—which was the control and broadcasting of news. Then came the day when she was called in to look at a strange body found in the arctic ice.

That was the first time she had ever seen a man.

At that instant, she realized several shocking truths . . . that she wasn't really happy, she wasn't really normal, her emotions were all unnatural, and her work wasn't free. It took a little while to discover the last, because she tried to broadcast the news—and ran headlong into a murderous censorship of whose very existence she had never dreamed.

From that moment on, her life and that of every other inhabitant of the world—all female—headed for the greatest crisis in history. The nature of that crisis, how the world got that way, and what would result, make up one of the most brilliantly *different* novels ever written.

CHARLES ERIC MAINE is a British author, now aged 36. A science-fiction fan of pre-war days, he served as a Signals Officer in the Royal Air Force during the war. His first success as a writer came in 1952 when his radio play *Spaceways* was a hit on the BBC, and subsequently was turned into a novel, a magazine serial, a motion picture, and a television drama. Other novels followed, among which are *Timeliner, The Isotope Man, Escapement, Crisis 2000, High Vacuum,* and *The Man Who Couldn't Sleep.* His work has appeared in both hard covers and paperbacks, and has been translated into Italian, Spanish, and Swedish.

He describes WORLD WITHOUT MEN as the book which he most enjoyed writing.

World Without Men

by
CHARLES ERIC MAINE

ACE BOOKS, INC.
23 West 47th Street, New York 36, N. Y.

PART ONE

THE MAN

I

AT PRECISELY nine o'clock the ultrasonic alarm sounded inaudibly in the bedroom. She awoke instantly and reached for the cup of hot coffee that had been delivered a few seconds earlier via the catering chute that connected her bedside table with the Central Provisioning Depot. She sipped the coffee, yawned a little, stretched languidly, then rose to face the routine of another day.

The bath was ready, with the water perfumed and preheated, and she immersed herself lazily, taking care not to splash her cropped black hair with its fresh coating of silicone varnish. In three minutes the detergents had cleaned the surface of her body, silently and invisibly, but she lingered on in the water until the advancing finger of the wall clock warned her that time was running out.

Back to the bedroom, and into a short white skirt and white sandals, then over to the long oval mirror beneath the sunglow lamp of the room. She examined her features critically. She was handsome enough in the tradition of the day. Her skin was smooth and burnished to a roseate bronze sheen, and the whites of her eyes had been stained green to contrast with the limpid brown of the pupils. She was not more than twenty-seven. Her name was Aubretia.

She studied her lips pensively, then selected the white cosmetic spray from the beauty table, and presently the pink bow shape of the lips became snow-white—to match her skirt. Her hair was satisfactory; the silicone varnish had been applied only three days ago and was good for another week. She wished sometimes that she had white hair, like Aquilegia; but then everything about Aquilegia was white, for she was an albino, and her pink eyes were the envy of every woman in the city.

The silver lacquer on her flat, atrophied breasts had worn thin in parts, but it would do. Later in the day she could visit the Beauty Center and have fresh lacquer applied—perhaps even a change of color. Silver was clean, but there were times when it resembled armor.

Satisfied with her appearance, she put the thick, purple collar around her neck, then pulled the snake-chain that dangled from it. The collar unrolled like a blind, dropping around her body to her ankles, veiling her in the fine gloss of a purple satin cloak She was ready to cope with another day's work.

The time was nine forty-five, time enough to walk the four blocks to the tall, columnar building of the State Biophysical Center. She turned towards the window, glancing briefly over the colorful spires of the skyline, glowing mystically in the morning sunshine. The thousands of seven and eight o'clockers would be there already, working and supervising in the slender buildings of the city; and the nine o'clockers would be picking up the threads of the day's executive duties; and soon the ten o'clockers, the administrative officials, would be arriving to keep an alert eye on the plans and schedules of the vast labor organization.

She left the apartment, descending to street level on the high-speed spiral escalator, then walked briskly with the other women wearing the authorized purple cloak of official-dom towards the parallel row of skyscrapers that housed the government offices.

The room had a sliding glass door bearing the legend: *Press Policy and Administration*. Inside was color and warmth and effeminacy: a large desk with slender legs, a dainty ivory table supporting an ornate crystal bowl of the newest kind of flowers that had been grown in phosphor nutrients so that the pentals glowed in luminous hues, graceful padded chairs, oval mirrors, and an arched window with stained glass panes in a variety of dilute rainbow colors. It was a woman's room in a woman's building in a woman's city.

Aubretia entered the office with a distinct sense of repose, almost of homecoming. The sensation was to formula, of course. It was part of the applied psychology of labor administration. Domestic apartments tended to be functional and austere while offices and factories were generally as comfortable and luxurious as applied science could make them. The result was increased productivity.

She pulled the snake-chain on her purple cloak. Immediately the garment coiled itself into a compact collar encircling her neck. She removed it and hung it on a peg behind the desk.

The pilot lamp on the memory bank unit was flashing green. She sat down and pressed the control button with a slim finger, then concentrated on the crisp impersonal voice of the recorder as it intoned the news messages of the night.

General release, said the voice. *Opening of new I. P. Center.* A brief pause. *Today at thirteen hundred hours the Mistress of Biogenetics will officially open the new I. P. Center at Lon South. The Center will specialize in the application and development of the latest techniques in the science of induced hetero-parthenogenesis with the object of increasing the variant factor of derivative types, which is not at present possible with normal auto-parthenogenetic methods.* Ten seconds of silence. *Electroscan pictures and detailed technical handouts will be distributed via authorized news agencies within twenty-four hours.*

A long pause. The memory bank unit whirred and clicked,

and a sheet of paper bearing a printed transcription of the message was deposited on the desk.

Restricted release, announced the voice a moment later. *For professional distribution to institutions and organizations in economic, financial, biogenetic, mortic and related fields: The government, following its recent biennial survey of mortic revenue assets, has decided to authorize an increase of two and a half per cent in live parthenogenetic births during the next two years as a preliminary to a statistical revision of the personal mortic tax assessment figure in the light of improving economic conditions. General release will follow in four days.*

Another pause—another sheet of printed paper.

General release: Entertainment news from Femina News Agency. State actress Butterfly II will star tonight in a video dramatic feature concerning the love of two adult women for a young albino girl whose parthenogenetic double becomes involved in a criminal attempt to . .

And so it went on, the usual small talk that passed for news, always with the accent on parthenogenesis and, curiously, albinos. *Signs of the times,* Aubretia thought. *After all, in a world where the majority of women were almost mirror images of each other there was a certain irrepressible fascination in albinos—if only because they were different.* A phantom image of Aquilegia hovered momentarily in her mind. Aubretia suppressed the inevitable emotional response almost before it had formed. Time enough to think about Aquilegia later in the day—in the long warm evening —but for all her resolution she spared a moment to acknowledge her pleasure and gratitude that she should be on such intimate terms with an albino.

And as for parthenogenesis, either in its auto or hetero forms, there was barely a single news item that did not refer to it in one way or another. It was one of the fundamentals of life—like eating, drinking and cremation, and it seemed sometimes as if the government were deliberately overemphasizing the importance of parthenogenesis in society. On the whole it was an unsavory subject. No woman voluntarily sought childbirth, either by natural or induced methods, and when it came it was invariably an ordeal to be undergone in the course of duty and for the sake of mortic allowances.

The voice of the memory bank droned on unheeded, and the sheets of printed paper piled up on the desk. In due course she would have to filter the news reports and pass them via the respective channels to the press and broadcasting agencies concerned. But the day was young, and there was still time to sit and dream in inactive idleness.

The monitor buzzed shrilly on the desk. She switched off the memory bank and keyed the intercom.

"Aubretia Two Seventeen," said the monitor. "Callardia Nine Fifty would like you to go down to the Biophysics Lab Annex right away, please."

Aubretia thought quickly. The woman known as Gallardia was Senior Cytologist in the Department of Physiology, a thick-set woman of square face and contact lenses over her yellow-stained eyes. A competent scientist, she had a cynical twist in her brain. What on earth could she want with the Press Policy Department?

"I'll be right down," Aubretia answered.

The Annex was four storys below, on the eighteenth floor of the Biophysics building. It was a small room adjoining the large laboratory, and it contained part of the equipment store together with a small refrigerated mortuary bank. In the laboratory itself a great deal of research into the physiological basis of parthenogensis was carried out, and the Annex was frequently used for specialized experimental work related to the field—the dissection of women, for instance, who during life had shown symptoms of aberration from the parthenogenetic norm.

Gallardia was waiting for her at the main door to the laboratory. Her square face seemed a little oblong, as if her chin had dropped with excitement.

"Ah, Aubretia!" she said, simmering. "You handle news."

Aubretia contrived to smile politely. "I don't handle it. I vet it."

Gallardia retracted her chin, and her face became square again. "Well, then, I've got something sensational for you to vet. This way."

She led the way through the laboratory to the Annex. Aubretia noted briefly the long benches and the glass and chrome apparatus and the technicians—some of them only young girls in their teens—wearing the approved-pattern, transparent plastic overalls. They continued into the smaller cube of the Annex, with its racks and shelves and cupboards and, in the center of the floor, an adjustable operating table with a sheeted body.

Gallardia placed a proprietary hand on the center of the body and regarded the other woman with an air of restrained triumph. "What would be the most fantastic event you could imagine?" she demanded

Aubretia spread out her hands noncommitally. "That's hard to say. A woman from Mars, perhaps?"

"Nonsense. We know there are no women on Mars."

"From out of space, then."

"No, no. That is fantasy. This"—she thumped the shape under the sheet—"is fact!"

"I really haven't the slightest idea."

"Then take a look." Gallardia drew back the sheet, revealing a white waxen head and shoulders.

"She's got a lot of hair," Aubretia observed. "Peculiar face too. Kind of hard. Ugly." Something caught her eye. She leaned forward quickly and inspected the dead face. "I could almost swear . . ."

"What?"

"More hair here, around the chin . . . like stubble."

Gallardia drew back the sheet a litle further. "And on the chest," she pointed out.

Aubretia retreated in mild revulsion.

"No breasts," Gallardia went on. "Only nipples of a rudimentary character."

"Then who is she? What's happened to her?" asked Aubretia, wide-eyed.

With a conjuror-like sweep of her arm, Gallardia removed the sheet altogether, revealing the full length of the naked corpse. "There!" she stated with evident satisfaction.

Aubretia was only conscious of certain grotesque detail. Her stomach seemed to contract and her abdomen to twist up inside itself. Her rational mind rejected the obvious explanation. Across a gap of five thousand years it was impossible, yet . . .

"It can't be!" she gasped in horror.

"But it is," Gallardia stated emphatically. "You are looking at a man!"

II

THE vaguely horrific image of the man stayed in Aubretia's mind for the remainder of the day. There was no sense of contact with humanity. Death in itself had created an invisible barrier behind which the corpse was no more than a bleached artifact crudely wrought in human shape, but different enough from womankind to be alien and remote. And with the image was a certain indefinable fear, not of the body in the Annex, but of something more fundamental, something that had to do with herself and Aquilegia and Gallardia, and all the women of the world. The fear was a shadow behind the shape of the man, not fully visible, yet significant in a chill way, darkening the perimeter of her consciousness with a sense of the unexplained.

Back in her office Aubretia struggled to recall Gallardia's terse description of the discovery of the body, and the anatomical and cytological evidence that proved beyond doubt the incredible fact of maleness. It was necessary to draft a report for submission to the Mistress of Information in the Department of the Written Word. The man was not yet public domain, and it was for the Mistress to determine whether the news could be released to the world.

It seemed that the Fourteenth Arctic Geophysical Expedition, while carrying out a radar survey of the ice layer close to the North Pole, had recorded a strong localized echo at a depth of some twenty-five feet below the surface. Further tests with spectrum analyzers had revealed a mass of metal in roughly cylindrical form, pointing downwards at a steep angle into the frozen mass of the polar cap. There were traces of aluminium and beryllium and copper, and, surprisingly, distinct evidence of radioactivity.

Thermonuclear heaters were then used to melt a funnel in the ice, and presently the members of the expedition uncovered the strange object. It was a rocket. This was an exciting discovery, for no rocket had been launched or even made on Earth for more than four thousand years. The earlier groping efforts at interplanetary flight had been quickly abandoned after preliminary radar and video surveys of the moon and the nearer planets by small robot rockets had revealed nothing to justify the enormous expenditure which an attempt to launch manned rockets across space would involve. It seemed more logical to womankind to devote worldly wealth on the development of the Earth and its inhabitants, and the feminine mind saw neither sense nor sanity in space travel.

But it was part of the mythology of history that men had taken the problem of interplanetary flight seriously. Nobody knew exactly when, for records were incomplete, but certainly many thousands of years ago. And this strange rocket buried in the polar ice was of a different pattern from those of the abortive rocket era in the age of women. It was straight and slender and functional. There were no little devices or artistic shaping of the hull fittings so characteristic of the feminine designer. A psychologist might have described its shape as phallic in origin, but there were no psychologists in the party, and, anyway, the word had been meaningless for some five thousand years.

The rocket was intact and sealed. It had been necessary to cut through the hull with arc-burners in order to gain access to the interior. Inside a tiny control cabin they had found the body, frozen solid, encased in a metal and plastic pressure suit.

The expedition had made no attempt to strip the body, partly because it was obviously dead, and partly because it was thought that the examination ought to be left to those whose job it was to deal with such matters. In due course the body and certain items of equipment from the rocket were flown back to civilization, where they were passed to the appropriate scientific departments concerned. Not a single woman in the expedition had even suspected that the body might be that of a man, despite the implication of the unfamiliar rocket design. Men were the last thing any woman would think of in this day and age.

The body had been removed from the pressure suit at the Aeronautical Research Center. The suit, it seemed, was of major interest, but the body, clothed in quaint attire which bore no parallel to any kind of wearing apparel in current use, was quickly disposed of by sending it intact to the Department of Biophysics. And so it reached the brusque efficient hands of Gallardia, who soon discovered that she had come into possession of a man, albeit a dead one.

The body was in a remarkably fine state of preservation,

probably due to the conditions of burial in ice during thousands of years. But now, no longer in deep freeze, it would obviously deteriorate rapidly unless the usual steps were taken. Gallardia was presumably working on it now, injecting formaldehyde into the veins and performing the preliminary evisceration. She had already made a cytological test of body cells and counted forty-seven chromosomes on the nuclei—positive proof of sex, if proof were needed.

There was nothing in the clothing to identify the man, only a few printed papers in a foreign language that neither Gallardia nor Aubretia could identify, and a gold ring on one finger of the corpse bearing the engraved letters. "R. D."

All this, of course, was the news story of the year, perhaps of the century. In a world in which the male sex had been abandoned by nature some five thousand years earlier as an unnecessary extravagance of evolution, the presence of a real man, even a dead one, was an item of profound interest. It was a stark reminder of prehistoric days when womankind existed at the level of the animals in the field, before nature had decided that a change was desirable in the mechanism by which the species could be perpetuated. It brought back the days when there were such things as men, now almost legendary creatures of a bygone mythology.

It was as if, for instance, they had found a cyclops. That's how real and unreal was the man in the Annex.

Aubretia switched on the videophone and dialed the number of the Department of the Written Word. Then she changed her mind and pressed the cancel button. This was something that would have to be discussed on a person-to-person basis. It was too important, and the videophone was too impersonal.

She put on her purple cloak, pulled the snake chain, and made her way to street level.

"The body will have to be erased without trace," stated

the Mistress of Information. Her eyes were expressionless and
her long triangular face was swarthy and serpentine. "There
is no need to look bewildered, my dear. I am merely reciting
government policy. All human remains identified as male are
incinerated without delay."

"But why?" asked Aubretia, not understanding. "Surely
the discovery of . . . of a man . . . is a matter of priority
news."

The Mistress of Information shook her head slowly. It was
the lethargic motion of a pendulum in the padded vastness of
the pastel office. "Please believe me when I say that it has
no news value whatever. I am not permitted to explain why.
So far as the contemporary world is concerned, the male sex
ceased to exist some five thousand years ago."

"I agree. That is recognized. But surely the body of a man
has some historic, some scientific value."

"None whatever."

The Mistress of Information stood up and walked idly
around the room, making no sound on the thick white pile
of the carpet. She moved like a phantom among the slender
fragile shapes of the furniture. Occasionally she glanced
obliquely at her visitor, but there was no warmth or sympathy
in her eyes, only a cold calculating shrewdness.

"There is such a thing," she said quietly, "as the parthenogentic adaptation syndrome. It has been a reality for five
thousand years and it determines the pattern of our life, of
our existence. We have to recognize its influence and comply with its requirements in terms of social behavior."

"I'm afraid I don't understand . . ."

"Then I'll try to explain, in so far as my terms of reference
will allow me. Long, long ago the human race was split into
two sexes—male and female—just as are the lower animals at
the present day. Sex, of course, is a mechanism designed to
achieve perpetuation of the species. More than that, it is a
mechanism whose purpose is to produce variants in the spe-

cies: By random admixture of the differing characteristics of
individual men and women, children were produced em-
bodying composites of those characteristics. Sometimes they
were mutants, offspring bearing new characteristics which
had emerged for the first time. The object of this undisci-
plined intermarriage of eugenic strains was to produce offspring of differing survival capacities."

"You mean," said Aubretia, "the survival of the fittest."

"Exactly. In other words—evolution. The germ cells of
both males and females carried the essential physical and
physiological characteristics of the individuals concerned in
the genes on the chromosomes in the nuclei of the cells. Marriage produced mixture. The chromosomes and the genes
were brought together. New permutations and combinations
of human anatomy and physiology arose at each birth. Some
were more suited to survival than others. In such a way, by
natural selection, nature sought to change the form of man,
slowly adapting him to his environment." The Mistress
smiled. "You will pardon me in using the word man in the
generic sense. I could just as well have said woman."

Aubretia nodded, feeling rather out of her depth. She was
beginning to acquire a new respect for her superior, and won-
dering just how much of what she was saying was factual,
and not merely a recital of governmental viewpoint.

"Natural selection, survival of the fittest, is the simple
mechanism of evolution, designed to adapt a living animal
to its environment, to ensure survival of the species. But
what happens when the animal concerned starts adapting
the environment to itself?"

Aubretia said nothing: she had nothing to say.

"Immediately, the evolutionary process of nature breaks
down. Natural selection no longer applies. Survival of the
fittest becomes obsolete. In fact, survival becomes the pre-
rogative of those who, by wealth and power, can mold their
environment to their own liking."

"All right," Aubretia murmured. "But what has all that to do with men?"

"There comes a time," the Mistress stated portentiously, "when nature begins to realize that the methods she employs are no longer suited to the conditions which apply. What is the point of producing variants when the fittest no longer survive, when those who survive are not necessarily the fittest? Variation and natural selection become meaningless. Sex as a variant technique becomes useless. Survival is determined by artificial factors: the ability to live in congenial surroundings, to buy the best medical aid, to reduce the labor of life by the acquisition of mechanical labor-saving devices, and so on."

"You talk about nature, but how could nature know?"

The Mistress raised an admonishing finger. "Nature is all wise. Towards the end of the twentieth century, when the development of unlimited atomic power completely negated the process of natural evolution, nature finally came to terms with the human race. Reproduction was still necessary, but variation was a waste of time and uneconomic."

"But why?"

"Consider: Five thousand years ago the population of the world was half male and half female. A billion men and a billion women. There you have a supreme example of the extravagance of nature."

"Extravagance?"

"Of course. One man could fertilize a thousand females—ten thousand in the course of a lifetime; yet nature provided an average of one man per woman. The result of such extravagance was sublimation of unexpended masculine drive in other spheres: war, faster and faster air and ground travel, interplanetary flight. The cosmos itself became a *mons Veneris* at which mankind as a whole set his cap."

Aubretia shifted uncomfortably on her chair. The trend of the conversation made her feel uneasy, aroused in her mind the same kind of dormant fear as had been instigated by the visual memory of the man. The whole subject was wrapped in a sinister cocoon of unfathomable mystery.

"I'd never realized," she said, "that men were so real. What I mean is that men have always been to me—to most women— a kind of legend, a fairy tale, or stories of ghosts and goblins."

"After five thousand years you could hardly expect more."

"Then why did men disappear so suddenly from the world?"

The Mistress sat down again at her desk, drumming her fingers lightly upon its shining surface. "It wasn't sudden. It was a slow process. The truth is they were no longer necessary. Evolution had ceased in the human species. Sexual variation was no longer necessary. So nature introduced an economy and eliminated the male sex."

"But how?"

"By adjusting the ratio of births so that more and more females were born. Eventually there were no male births whatever. And at the same time parthenogenesis developed into a natural function of the female sex."

"I suppose it's logical," Aubretia conceded. "After all, if women can have children without the—the intervention of a male, then there seems to be no point in having two sexes."

"Exactly. And the beauty of it is this. The female ovum contains twenty-four chromosomes. By parthenogensis, whether natural or induced, the ovum splits into a normal cell of forty-eight chromosomes: a *female* cell. It is absolutely impossible to produce a healthy male cell of forty-seven chromosomes by parthenogenesis. Obviously, then, woman is the end product of nature. Man was merely an interim stage incapable of perpetuation other than by heterosexual means. You see, the male gametes were divided into two parts: those with twenty-three chromosomes and those with twenty-four, formed by subdivision of the forty-seven chromosomes in his body cells."

"I understand now," said Aubretia. "In order to produce a male child you must have a gamete with twenty-three chromosomes combining with a female ovum of twenty-four. Otherwise the product is always female."

The Mistress smiled triumphantly. "Exactly. That was the card nature had up her sleeve. The fundamental permanence of the female and the transcience of the male." She stroked her cropped black hair with a long, slender finger. "With the elimination of the male sex the possibility of producing male offspring became nil. Parthenogenesis can only produce females."

"When did parthenogenesis really start?" Aubretia asked.

"That's difficult to say. There were isolated cases throughout the ages. Seven thousand years ago there was a well-authenticated case of a parthenogenetic individual called Christ; but towards the end of the twentieth century it increased immeasurably, and at the same time men died off."

Aubretia considered for a moment, reviewing all that she had learned. "The adaptation you mentioned," she said. "Where does that fit in?"

The Mistress smiled for the first time, a confident knowledgeable smile. "A sex may disappear according to the dictates of nature, but the endocrine structure of the female body remains the same."

"Endocrine?"

"The ductless glands—the hormones. They are the basis of emotional feeling. The emotions have not changed, but they *have* been modified."

Aubretia pursed her lips thoughtfully. "Emotions I know about, but how have they been modified?"

The Mistress paused for a moment, choosing her words carefully. "Whom do you love?" she enquired.

"An albino woman named Aquilegia," Aubretia said, with a certain degree of self-consciousness.

"Then it may surprise you to know that there was a time when women needed men, when women loved men."

"No!" Aubretia gasped incredulously.

"It is true. But during the course of five thousand years an emotional transfer has taken place, from necessity. Now women need and love each other."

"But surely that is natural. Women are the same; they know about each other."

The Mistress shook her head sadly. "I'm afraid you're missing the point because you can't see the point. That is as it should be. An adaptation has taken place, a fundamental reorganization of the emotional architecture of womankind. But perhaps you can appreciate that it would be undesirable, perhaps even dangerous, to introduce a conflicting element. It would be fatal to introduce the idea of man because there is a chance, just the slight chance, that some women might respond to it—those women who have not quite conformed to the emotional pattern of the adaptation syndrome. That is why the male body in the Annex must be destroyed."

Aubretia remained silent for fully a minute. She was trying to understand things from two independent and divorced points of view. Primarily she was a citizen of a female world, living and existing within a circumscribed pattern of emotional behavior in accordance with what the Mistress termed the parthenogenetic adaptation syndrome; but in addition she was also a woman, and the man still hovered ghost-like in the depth of her mind, hinting at a different level of being beyond her imagination, a level that was simultaneously repulsive and fascinating, that tugged at her imagination and created strange transient sensations in her body that differed in some subtle way from the orgastic feelings that Aquilegia and her predecessors had aroused.

"I'll tell you something," the Mistress continued in confidential tones. "This is not the first man to be discovered. There have been many during the past millennia, hundreds upon hundreds. Some were well preserved, some were mere crumbling skeletons. But they have all been destroyed. The syndrome must be preserved at all costs if the stable basis of modern society is to be preserved."

The Mistress stood up with an air of finality. "There will be no news release, and I shall make arrangements immediately for the body to be incinerated. As a servant of the government you will, of course, have nothing to say on the subject to anyone. The man is a secret, dead *or* alive, an obscene secret of ancient history."

Aubretia bowed understandingly and took her leave.

III

AQUILEGIA was a woman in high key. She was a vision in pale cream against a background of white. She lived in the top apartment of one of the highest apartment blocks in Lon North and she was lightness itself, like the sky. The rooms of her home were decorated in the palest of pastel hues, and the furniture was mainly of transparent plastic material. In this setting of whiteness and semi-invisibility she was an object of slender fragile beauty, pure in her whiteness and almost intangible in her ethereal albinism.

She was wearing a gossamer gown in spider latex. It was white, in the translucent white of spun glass, but no whiter than the flesh it concealed. Only the nipples were darker under the folds of the garment, smoke-tinted, diminutive, and the body hair was colorless. Her fingernails and toenails were lacquered in silver, and her lips were ivory-white with cosmetic. The pink of her eyes was generously extended by means of suitably matched stain over the entire surface of the cornea, lending her a transcendental air of remote ghostliness. But for all that she was as real and as physical as any woman Aubretia had ever known.

They sat on a colorless veranda looking out over the twinkling multicolored lights of the city in the fading daylight.
They were drinking ambrosia, which, according to the label
on the bottle, was ninety proof. Blue gin, Aquilegia called it,
and blue it was, with a kind of phosphorescent midsummer
blueness.

"Relax," Aquilegia whispered, stroking the bare arm of
her companion. Aubretia sank deeper into the soft resilience
of her chair, allowing herself to be soothed.

"I'm sure you take your job too seriously," Aquilegia went
on. "And if you do that, well, you're putting mortic revenue
at too high a level."

"Quilly," breathed Aubretia, "this has nothing to do with
mortic revenue. But, God, I'm glad I came to see you tonight.
I need something to settle my mind."

For a moment they kissed, a cool lingering kiss. The descending darkness deepened and the city lights gleamed more
brightly.

"Quilly," said Aubretia, "I've a problem on my mind. I
can't talk about it, yet I feel I need to talk about it. But if
I talk then I'm committing an official crime."

"You don't have to tell me unless you want to, darling."

"I know, Quilly. Perhaps in the ordinary way I wouldn't
have mentioned it at all, but somebody we both know is concerned. I really don't know what to do . . . which way to
turn. . . ."

"Who is concerned?"

"Someone you knew when you worked in the Department
of Biophysics."

"Euphorbia?"

"No."

"Criniflora?"

"No."

"Then who?"

Aubretia took her friend's hand and squeezed it warmly.

"I really shouldn't tell you, but, well, you're different, Quilly. I know I can trust you. It's Gallardia. She's disappeared."

Aquilegia turned her pink eyes towards Aubretia. "What do you mean 'disappeared'?"

"I'm not sure. You know what Gallardia is like: blunt, a little outspoken. She was working on the body, and I've got a feeling she refused to co-operate."

"Co-operate with whom?"

"With the government, the Mistress of Information. You see, Quilly, she was working on the body of a man."

Aquilegia's pink eyes widened for an instant. She lifted the bottle of ambrosia and refilled the two glasses. "You said a man," she prompted.

"For God's sake, Quilly," Aubretia said, "keep this to yourself. They found the body of a man, in good condition. Gallardia was working on it, and I was called in to handle the press story. But the Department of the Written Word thought otherwise. I talked with the Mistress of Information, and she killed the story, said she would have the body destroyed. When I got back to the Biophysics Lab., Gallardia had gone."

"Tell me, Aubry," Aquilegia asked, "did you see this—this man?"

Aubretia nodded.

"You're quite sure it *was* a man?"

"How would I know? I can only judge by what I saw."

"And the body is to be destroyed."

"Yes. That was the part I found difficult to accept. The Mistress tried to explain . . . something about an adaptation syndrome."

Aquilegia smiled enigmatically and refilled the glasses with ambrosia. "When you say Gallardia had gone, what exactly do you mean? Did she leave of her own free will or was she abducted?"

"I don't know, Quilly. The lab assistants say she left with the mortic people who removed the body."

"And why are you worried about her?"

Aubretia hesitated. The blue gin was beginning to seep into her brain and coherent thought was becoming difficult. "I think it was the way the Mistress of Information talked, about the need for secrecy, and so on. You know what Gallardia is like; she couldn't keep a secret for more than ten seconds."

Aquilegia smiled without moving her lips. "I don't think you need worry about her," she said quietly. "You will not see her again, but she will be well and safe."

Aubretia regarded her companion questioningly, noting subconsciously the unexpected manifestation of hard poise beneath the sweetness of her form and coloring.

"The Department of the Written Word is closely associated with the Department of Social Stability. They have a common policy on matters that affect the P.A.S.," Aquilegia added.

"P.A.S.?"

"Parthenogenetic Adaptation Syndrome."

"What has that to do with Gallardia?"

Aquilegia spread out her hands noncommittally. "Very little, really. She has certain information that could, conceivably, conflict with the syndrome if it were spread around. The information must be erased." A pause while she sipped her drink, watching Aubretia with expressionless pink eyes. "Don't be alarmed, darling. Gallardia will come to no harm. It is a mere matter of what we might call hynotic technique, a slight remodelling of the cerebral memory tracks by induced suggestion. Afterwards she will remember nothing of the man. She will almost certainly be transferred to another laboratory in a remote part of the country."

Aubretia stood up slowly, holding her glass, and leaned against the low railing of the verandah. The cavernous streets of the city yawned eighteen storys below, but her eyes were on her friend, and there was a certain quality of constraint in her poise which defied the creeping flaccidity of her limbs as the gin permeated her blood.

"You seem to know a great deal about departmental policy and procedure, Quilly. I never realized you had any contact with the government—not to that extent."

The other woman's smile seemed warm and genuine enough. "Don't get worried, darling. I know a great deal that perhaps I shouldn't know. I've got an inquiring mind."

"What else do you know?"

"That you're a beautiful and desirable woman. There, does that make you feel better?"

"Should it?"

Again the enigmatic gloss in the pale pink eyes. A faint sense of alarm clutched icily at Aubretia's heart. She returned to her seat and finished her drink, then touched Aquilegia's arm with nervous fingers.

"Quilly, you're not getting fed up with me, are you?"

"Of course not, darling. I'm teasing you, really. Tell me, when the Mistress of Information talked about the syndrome, did you understand her?"

"Vaguely. It had to do with evolution. How women had adapted themselves to parthenogentic existence without men. Then she said something about modifying the emotions."

Aquilegia nodded soberly. "Do you feel that your emotions have been modified?"

"Of course not."

"Life seems perfectly normal to you: life and love and parthenogenesis?"

"Yes, Quilly. Shouldn't it?"

"The Mistress of Information told you that the male sex died off because they were no longer necessary."

"Yes. She said nature had found there was no further need for variants because we had learned how to adapt the environment to ourselves. Men died out and parthenogenesis came in."

Aquilegia filled the glasses again with a steady hand. "Did she say when parthenogenesis started."

"Not exactly. There have been isolated cases throughout history. A parthenogentic woman called Christ, for instance, some seven thousand years ago."

"Christ was a man," Aquilegia pointed out.

Aubretia considered this for a moment, sipping her drink thoughtfully. "That's impossible; a man has forty-seven chromosomes and you can't produce a male by parthenogenesis."

"Nevertheless, Christ was a man."

"Then he couldn't have been parthenogenetic."

"Exactly, Aubry. He couldn't have been. Did the Mistress quote any more known cases of natural parthenogenesis?"

"No."

"And today, five thousand years after the disappearance of man from the face of Earth, how many women achieve natural childbirth by parthenogenesis?"

Aubretia ran the tip of her little finger around the contour of her chin, vaguely aware that the conversation was becoming too deep for her. "The majority," she stated, but without conviction.

"Have you seen the statistics?"

"No. Not recently."

Aquilegia smiled sardonically. "Have you ever seen any statistics at all?"

"Not as such. But there have been numerous official statements for the press . . ."

"From the Department of the Written Word, no doubt inspired by the Department of Social Stability. I'll tell you something Aubry: There aren't any statistics. At least, not the kind that you or I could see. Such figures as are recorded are top secret and are kept under lock and key."

Aubretia gripped her glass with fingers that trembled slightly, and drained the blue liquid in a single fiery gulp. The fairy lights of the city in the precipitating gloom danced hazily beyond focus. Aquilegia's face was a smooth white mask in the darkness.

"Would it surprise you to learn that there are no natural parthenogenetic births whatever?" Aquilegia continued. "There never have been. Possibly one or two cases in ten million that cannot be authenticated anyway."

"Quilly!" gasped Aubretia. "You can't be serious."

"But I am, darling."

"But the live birth quota of hundreds of babies every day by parthenogenesis."

"*Induced* parthenogenesis, Aubry, simply applied cytology. The ovum is persuaded to divide and subdivide and develop without fertilization, by *artificial* means."

Aubretia stood up again, swaying slightly, and leaned against the balcony railing, holding it tightly with one hand. "That's not true. Four years ago I had two babies by natural parthenogenesis."

"How do you know? In this age of disease-free living any one of the prophylactic injections we have periodically could be a parthenogenetic stab. The rest follows automatically."

"They wouldn't dare. It would be an infringement of personal liberty."

"That's rather a platitude for you, Aubry. In point of fact we haven't any personal liberty; we are 'free' only in so far as we comply with the adaptation syndrome. And *that* is something of a misnomer. It isn't a syndrome at all. It's a pattern of behavior enforced from outside. We're conditioned—all of us."

Aubretia sighed, and placed her empty glass on the table. "I've never heard you talk this way before, Quilly. It alarms me. It's not as if there were any evidence for what you say.

I was never conditioned. Nobody forced a pattern of behavior on *me*. I just can't believe it."

"But you were born and raised in a State nursery and educated at a State dispersal college, weren't you, Aubry? That's when they conditioned you—when your mind was young and flexible. And they erased the memories you weren't supposed to have by deep hypnotic control."

"But for what purpose?"

There was an interval of silence in the darkness. Both women were pallid ghostly forms, quite motionless. The colored lights of the city reflected in tiny clusters from the surface of the ambrosia bottle and the curved glasses on the table.

Presently Aquilegia said: "I'm sorry, Aubry. I think perhaps I've been talking too much, and I can see I'm confusing you. Let's forget about it for now. Perhaps we'll pick up some other time."

"No," Aubretia insisted. "I want to know what all this is about. What are you trying to prove."

"Nothing at all, darling. Nothing that can make any difference to us."

"It has something to do with the man."

"Forget about the man. He's probably been reduced to smoke and ashes by now."

Something in the tone of her friend's voice arrested Aubretia's attention. She saw the dead naked body of the man in her mind's eye. "You *know* something, Quilly," she stated. "The man hasn't been destroyed at all; is that it?"

"All right," Aquilegia said wearily. "He hasn't been destroyed. He's in cold storage in a secret underground laboratory outside Lon, along with hundreds of other dead men. But don't ask me how I know or why. It's a long story and I'm tired, and so are you. Let's go to bed, darling."

"All right," Aubretia murmured reluctantly. "But I shan't sleep."

"I don't want you to sleep. . . . Not for a long time," said
Aquilegia.

She led the way from the dark veranda into the room,
switching on the light. From there, arm in arm, slightly
drunk, they walked slowly into the bedroom.

IV

THE next day Aubretia suffered from an increasing sense of
restlessness. The blue gin had obliterated most of her memory of the previous night, and only the outline of her conversation with Aquilegia remained, a blank silhouette without detail. But there was disquietude beneath the surface
of her mind. She found it difficult to concentrate on routine
work.

Early in the morning she called in at the biophysics laboratory for news of Gallardia, but there was none. Her place
had been taken by an immense, florid woman of indeterminate age, with glossy inflexible features that had probably
been rejuvenated by plastic surgery. The Annex was empty,
and it was as if the man had never existed.

The news releases of the night, stored in the memory
bank, were unsensational. A giant sunspot was disrupting
intercontinental radio communications; an elderly woman in
China had produced parthenogenetic triplets (a minor miracle of applied cytology, Aubretia recognized); car exports
were up by nearly one per cent on the previous year; and the
government had modified one of the regulations concerning
mortic revenue to stimulate voluntary induced parthenogenesis in older women. It was the formula as before, with the
accent always on childbirth, whether artificial or induced.

But, according to Aquilegia (and Aubretia remembered
this distinctly) there was no such thing as natural parthenogenesis. It was a myth, a fiction designed to cover up syste-

matic induction by subterfuge. She surveyed briefly the many
clinical prophylactics required by law during the course of a
year: the antibiotics and the antivirus serums, the anticarcino-
genic injections, the antisenility drugs and the gynotropic
stimulants on which the extended romantic life of the community depended. It was feasible—indeed, practicable—that
one of the many compulsory hypodermics considered necessary to modern health and hygiene might contain a parthenogenetic factor, a drug that would induce division and subsequent fertile development of the quiescent ovum. There was
no possible way in which the ensuing pregnancy could be
differentiated from any hypothetical case of natural parthenogenesis.

She recalled her own experiences in the State Maternity
Center, the two long and boring pregnancies (ostensibly of
natural origin) which she had endured in a quiet spirit of
conscientious duty. She sometimes wondered vaguely about
the two children whom she had never seen. They would be
five and six years old now, alike as photostats, resembling
herself in every detail, and undergoing the assembly line education of the State Institute at one of the many giant schools
dispersed throughout the country. Children she would never
know, and, if it came to the point, children with whom she
could one day unwittingly have a love affair. Such was the
complex structure of modern society determined by the adaptation syndrome, or by hypnotic cerebral conditioning—whatever you liked to call it.

Resentment filtered slowly into her mind, a vague unspeci-
fied resentment without form or orientation. And with it came
the realization that her executive post of responsibility was
neither executive nor responsible, was no more than a minute
reflexing component in a vast automation network of synthetic news and propaganda. She was a human relay, a robot
agent detailed to pass on authorized news to the main press
and broadcast information channels, and a safeguarding

filter to query items of suspect news value, items such as the man.

She tore a piece of paper from a pad on the desk and wrote on it with a graphomatic stylus. *Scientific democracy.* Her handwriting was small and neat, but sloped irregularly across the page. *Freedom within the State.* A pause while she gathered her thoughts. What did that mean? Freedom to conform with the requirements of the State? The square-jowled features of the Mistress of Information stared hollowly into the dark recesses of her mind. *There will be no news release, and I shall make arrangements immediately for the body to be incinerated.* Freedom to do as you are told by government officials.

Aquilegia's voice echoed faintly within her brain. *He hasn't been destroyed. He's in cold storage in a secret underground laboratory.*

But why? For what purpose? In a world of women where man was an obsolete device from ancient history, what was the point of Aquilegia's statement?

She replaced the graphomatic on the desk and stared vacantly at the luminous flowers on the spindly table. Aquilegia was, a trusted friend: she couldn't be entirely wrong. The government and the State were not all they seemed to be on the surface. News was being suppressed to fit a pattern, an unimaginable pattern with an unimaginable purpose.

"To hell with it!" she said aloud. The suspicion and uncertainty had to be resolved once and for all. An imp of mischief began to spin and whirl and twist in her brain, inspired and stimulated by the hangover factor of the blue gin in her system. She was the Press Policy and Administration Officer, wasn't she? Surely the title implied that she was competent to originate policy and determine the nature of administration without continual reference to the Department of the Written Word. Surely she had the right to use her own discretion.

She switched on the videophone and dialed 'B'. The broadcast pilot lamp flashed three times. She paused uncertainly, uncomfortably aware that what she was about to say would be recorded by memory banks in every newspaper office and television newsroom in the land. And, more ominously, on the monitor bank in the office of the Mistress of Information.

She dictated slowly. "General release. The body of a man in well-preserved condition has been discovered buried deep in the polar ice by the Fourteenth Arctic Geophysical Expedition. After a preliminary examination the body has been removed to a secret laboratory for further research."

A pause—five seconds.

"Statistics show that there are virtually no natural parthenogenetic births. All births are induced surreptitiously . . ."

A red light winked on the video control panel. The circuit went dead. She realized abruptly that her broadcast had been cut off by a master circuit. Pale and motionless she waited for the inevitable noise of the videophone buzzer. It came ten seconds later.

She pressed the contact button. The square face of the Mistress of Information peered at her from the small screen.

"Don't move," said the Mistress. "And don't worry. You will be all right. We shall come for you in about two minutes."

They came in one minute and forty seconds.

Birm was a beautiful city, in many ways more beautiful than Lon. It was more spacious, and the air seemed cleaner and fresher. From her apartment Aubretia could look down a wide tree-lined avenue that receded to a hazed horizon four or five miles away. Vehicles more than twenty storys below crawled along the highway like tiny multicolored beetles. The buidings were slender ethereal columns of chrome, white concrete and glass, and at night they were outlined in rainbow neon.

She had been doing the new job for several weeks now, and on the whole she preferred the change. The work, which had to do with the collating and filing of governmental statistical records, was less exacting than press liaison, even if more monotonous. Sometimes she wondered why she had applied for the transfer, but it was always difficult to isolate a precise reason. At all events she had asked, and the government had obliged.

She had a friend called Valinia who worked in the same department as herself. Valinia was a lithe olive-skinned girl, not more than twenty-three, with a firm shapely body and a comprehensive fund of erotic knowledge that bewildered and fascinated Aubretia. By coincidence Valinia lived in the apartment immediately below Aubretia's and before long they spent most of their leisure time together. It wasn't a question of love—the emotional contact didn't go that deeply—but rather a matter of physical and emotional captivation. There were times when Aubretia suspected that her new friend's attitude was a little too calculating and predetermined, but the suspicion never survived the erotic impact of Valinia's alluring presence.

Life was very smooth and easy, not only for Aubretia herself but for womankind as a whole. Many of the more comprehensible statistics and computations that passed through her hands confirmed the general conditions of well-being and prosperity in which human affairs thrived. In a sense everything was tied to the industrial production program throughout the world. Vast factories turned out the requirements of civilization without staff, without workers, powered by atomic energy, controlled by automation, and remotely supervised by wired television units. The arteries of supply and provision were healthy and abundantly used. The labor program was, therefore, mainly concerned with the supervision of machines and the balancing of productivity against needs. For

more than a thousand years the balance had been maintained
with a fine accuracy.

There had, of course, been little progress in the sense of
absolute research; indeed, certain fields of technological in-
vestigation had even retrogressed. Astronautics, for example,
was a dead subject. Rockets were no longer made apart from
a few small projectiles used for meteorological purposes. Aircraft design had not altered within living memory, perhaps
not even in millennia. The high-powered stratojets that could
circle the earth in twenty-four hours without refueling were
adequate for all purposes. In the field of atomic engineering,
research had halted once the production of nuclear power
had been established on an economic basis. It was the female
viewpoint, essentially practical and in no way visionary,
using techonology for what it could give with no interest in
abstract research for its own sake, that prevailed.

The same practical attitude had resolved the major problems of power politics. Although womankind was still split
by geographical divisions into independent continental
groups, there was close liaison at every level of life and work.
The separate governing bodies were co-ordinated by a central committee which was franchised to act in an advisory
capacity on all questions of governing policy and local administration. It was recognized that government was part of
the regulating machinery of society, an enormous ductless
gland controlling the basic functioning of the organism as a
whole, but it was the organism which was important, not
the gland.

Nor had women bothered to theorize about their science or
society. Some called it a scientific democracy, others a tech-
nocracy, and still others a controlled anarchy. The names
meant nothing: The mechanism functioned just as efficiently
whatever the label applied to it.

This state of relative Utopia had materialized slowly during
the past five thousand years. There was a feeling, which

Aubretia shared, that it had come about as a result of the disappearance of man from the earth. Although little was known of man and the kind of world in which he held sway, the Department of the Written Word had pointed out on many occasions that the wars and political disputes of past ages were undoubtedly characteristic of the male sex. One had only to consider the lower animals (in which male-female differentiation still existed) to appreciate the fundamental difference between the psycho-physical behavior pattern of the two sexes. There never could have been a Utopia while man survived and controlled human affairs, for his innate aggressiveness and insatiable curiosity forced him restlessly to pursue the ever-widening boundary of knowledge without giving a thought to the application of his newly found powers in the service of humanity. In abolishing man, nature had opened the way to the permanent establishment of peace and plenty. Several women scientists had pointed out that man had been necessary to nature's purpose; he had tackled, with considerable energy and ingenuity, the problem of adapting his environment to himself, and had succeeded in wresting from the blind forces of the cosmos all the power he needed to secure the supremacy and ultimate survival of the human race as an entity. And at that point man became redundant. Worse he became an obstacle to the wise and peaceful exploitation of natural power for the benefit of his species. So man ceased to exist, and woman became mistress of her planet, and nature provided parthenogenesis to replace the outmoded reproduction mechanism that had vanished with the male sex.

It was a clear, logical and satisfactory picture. Everything seemed to be on the credit side, with one or two minor debits that were doubtless necessary if unpleasant. The first and by far the most disquieting, so far as Aubretia was concerned, was the mode of taxation employed throughout the world, for, of course, the benefits of social prosperity and stability

had to be paid for by those who enjoyed it. The Department
of Mortic Revenue was a term that always chilled her mind
and heart whenever she heard it mentioned, or even thought
about it. The word mortic was a polite euphemism; what they
meant was death. It was the word which pinpointed the entire mechanism of the tax system and, incidentally, gave a
clue to the means by which population level was controlled
and kept within the limits proscribed by the parameters of
industrial productivity.

She discussed the subject with Valinia one evening after
having read during the day a statistical report which stated
that the number of mortic revenue deaths below the age of
forty-five had increased by nearly seven per cent during the
past year. Mortic revenue deaths was another way of saying
compulsory euthanasia. It was, in a sense, the exact opposite
of parthenogenetic births, and the two were strictly balanced. Birth and death rates always increased or decreased
in exact proportion.

"At one time," said Aubretia, "the question of mortic law
never entered my head at all. But now that I'm growing
older I find myself thinking about it more and more, and it
seems to me that the taxation side is only a small part of it."

Valinia regarded her with bright brown eyes. "Why should
you worry, Aubry? The mortic tax assessors must be quite
happy with your record."

"I'm not worried. It's just that, well, it seems to me that
this business of mortics is the only unpleasant thing in a very
pleasant world."

Valinia laughed lightly. "It's the old story of day and
night, light and dark. You can't have one without the other.
Besides, the arrangement is much more satisfactory and
efficient than the old obsolete systems of taxation. At one
time the machinery of State revenue became so complex that
it took five years for tax assessors to learn their job and
everybody had to employ an accountant because the rules

and regulations were beyond human comprehension. There's the eugenic angle, too."

"That's what I mean. I'm beginning to think the eugenic side is more important than the revenue."

"There isn't any revenue, Aubry. It's all on paper, a computation by an electronic brain. Productivity and service is the real monetary system of the tax, and that's where the eugenic element comes in."

Aubretia abandoned the discussion for a while and scanned a picture magazine, but the three-dimensional color photographs were uninteresting. Even the nude stills of the erotic dancer known as Luella III, who was reputed to have the longest legs and the widest thighs in the Western hemisphere, failed to attract a second glance. Valinia had considerably more essential erotic fire in the touch of her little finger.

Presently her mind disassociated itself from the pages of the magazine and returned to the darker problem of mortics. She considered the basic principle: that all individuals from birth have a certain monetary value to the State, based on the service they render and the productivity they can achieve in terms of work. At the moment of birth a woman might have an immense potential value, for her future achievements were unknown; at the instant of death, however, her value was nil, for her service to the State had come to a stop. Between those two extremes lay a lifetime of labor and applied effort, mental or physical, that formed the basic economic unit of a functioning society.

Translating the abstract into the concrete was a complex matter, and the Department of Mortic Revenue had solved the problem to some extent by devising arbitrary standards. There was, for instance, the fundamental unit assessment. Every individual, and every child at birth, had a price on her head, an assessment in terms of dollars based on the average expected productivity of any single citizen. Nobody knew the exact figure. It varied from year to year, depending on the economic climate of the State and the world as a whole. But it might, for instance, be eight hundred thousand dollars. The figure was carefully calculated by a bank of electronic computors in a secret government department.

The general theory, as Aubretia understood it, was that during a normal lifetime (eighty years, according to the Statistical Division of the Department of Mortic Revnue) a normal citizen should, without undue self-sacrifice, be able to provide eight hundred thousand dollars worth of service or productivity for the benefit of the State. She was, however, rather vague about what would happen if the hypothetical citizen failed to attain her target, or, on the other hand, exceeded it. And it seemed to her that Valinia, whose knowledge of governmental administration was apparently as profound as her grasp of erotic techniques, might be able to clarify some of the more obscure points.

"Valy," she said, jettisoning the magazine, "when you said just now that there isn't any revenue, what exactly did you mean?"

Valinia, who had been watching the video screen in a desultory fashion, collected her thoughts and said, "Perhaps that wasn't quite accurate. Suppose I pay you to do a job for me, do I get any revenue out of it?"

"Well . . . no."

"But you do."

"Yes."

Valinia smiled subtly. "You're wrong, Aubry. If I pay you to do a job, then it is a principle of human labor relations that the job is worth more to me than I pay to you. The revenue comes to me. It isn't in money, but in service. That's the basic principle of mortic revenue, and it's the only kind of revenue that matters in the last analysis. Service and productivity."

"But supposing a citizen is unproductive and opposed to service."

"The same rules apply, Aubry. Antisocial types have the same tax assessment as normal citizens, but they suffer in a number of obvious ways. In the first place the salary they are permitted to draw from the State depends entirely upon their service or productivity factor. Those who work hard can draw more money so that they enjoy a higher standard of living. The shirkers draw less, and their standard of living is obviously lower.

"I see. It's a sort of self-balancing arrangement. But I still can't understand how the tax operates."

Valinia stroked her legs idly. "It's quite simple, Aubry. Everyone has an assessment. If they fail to produce or serve to the value of the assessment then they are in debt to the State. The figures are computed by electronic brains for every individual. If I were idle, for example, the State might assume that I was unproductive to the extent of, say, twenty thousand dollars."

Aubretia tried to understand, but the concept eluded her probing mind. "How could you possibly repay that amount?" she asked.

"By working harder."

"But suppose you didn't want to work harder; suppose you preferred to exist as a parasite."

"In that case the State would readjust the only other variable in order to balance the mortic revenue assessment. Life itself."

Aubretia stared at her friend a little aghast, not fully understanding.

"You mean that the State would destroy the nonproductive individuals?"

"Not the State, darling, the Department of Mortic Revenue. Every individual must fulfill her mortic assessment on a pro rata basis. The productive types live long and draw high salaries. The antisocial types draw low salaries and live a short, idle life. Their length of life is proportional to their productive capacity. For example, a woman who is euthanased at thirty will be found to have a service factor that could not produce more than three hundred thousand dollars worth of productivity during an average eighty year lifetime."

Aubretia began to walk around the room, conscious of a certain sensation of doubt and misgiving. "It seems to me," she observed, "that the State tends to regard life as a kind of mathematical equation: dollars versus productivity."

"Why not?"

"I don't really know. It just seems wrong in principle."

Valinia stood up, smiling, and came over to Aubretia, putting her arms around her affectionately. Aubretia was conscious of the warmth of her body. Her sensual acuity sharpened. She responded warmly, stroking her friend's arm.

Valinia said: "The State has to deal with nearly one hundred million women in this country alone. It has to deal with figures on a statistical basis. The whole basis of mortic revenue is to provide individuals with a strong incentive to become good citizens, to give service and to be productive. The standard required is moderate. You and I and millions of others can attain it quite easily. Those who fail are those who are least useful to all of us, to society as a whole: the idle and lazy people, the criminals, the subversive types, the political intriguers. All these tend to undermine the stability of our way of life. Do you understand, Aubry?"

Aubretia nodded slowly. The abstract problems of mortic revenue were beginning to evaporate and they no longer seemed important in Valinia's vital presence. Valinia came closer to her until her lips were a fraction of an inch away. They kissed.

"You worry too much, darling," Valinia murmured.

Aubretia said nothing.

"Let's forget about mortic revenue," Valinia whispered intimately. "It can't affect either of us ever."

"That's what I've been worrying about, Valy. For a long time there's been something at the back of my mind, something buried and forgotten, and I can't help feeling it has to do with mortics."

Valinia smiled. "You're crazy, Aubry."

"Yes, I must be."

"About me."

"Mm."

Valinia seized her partner possessively. Aubretia sighed gently and squeezed Valinia's arm.

Aubretia followed her out of the room.

V

THE weeks passed by smoothly, in a routine pattern, hazy and pleasurable. The world was kind and beautiful in its own unchanging way. The world was Valinia and beyond her was the rest of womankind, shadows against a mellow golden backdrop that was contemporary society. Life was a relationship between two people, and the relationship was warm and fruitful and reassuring. Even the morbid problem of mortic revenue clicked suddenly into a more comforting perspective, for she realized that control of death was just as logical as control of birth; indeed, the two were an intimately related function of the balanced state. And there was satisfaction in the thought that by a long term process of selection and elimination the human race itself would inevitably be improved, both physically and spiritually.

Then, one evening, the unexpected happened. Valinia had gone to Lon for three days on some vague government assignment, and Aubretia was alone in her apartment, missing the solace of her friend's company, but making the best of

what entertainment the video system had to offer. At nine
o'clock the doorbell intoned a solemn chime.

Aubretia opened the door and found herself face to face
with Aquilegia. There was no instant shock of recognition.
She was initially aware of an albino face and dark subdued
clothing, and it seemed to her that the face was familiar. It
was a face that had impressed itself on her memory at some
remote instant in time past.

"Aubry," breathed the visitor. "Remember me?"

Aubretia stared for a few moments, her mind quite blank
but racing wildly through patterns of recollection and asso-
ciation to no avail. Recognition was concealed behind an
elusive dark barrier in the unexplored depths of her consciousness.

"I'm Aquilegia," said the albino woman urgently. "I must
come in."

Aubretia stood aside, closing the door behind the intruder.

"Lock it, please."

She locked the door, not understanding why, but fascinated by the pale waxen skin and the pink eyes of the other
woman.

Aquilegia removed her drab gray cloak. The short white
skirt she wore beneath was creased and dirty. The white
lacquer that had covered her breasts had cracked and peeled
here and there. Her hair was longer and more tangled than
taste permitted. She looked like a hunted woman.

"Who did you say you are?" Aubretia asked.

Aquilegia's eyes became morose and melancholy. "Then
you don't recognize me, Aubry. That's what I was afraid of.
They did a good job on you, didn't they?"

Aubretia sat down, motioning her visitor to an adjacent
chair. "Should I know you?" she enquired.

Aquilegia smiled ruefully. "We were lovers once, only a
few months ago."

"But that's impossible."

"Please believe me; it's true. You don't remember it because the memory has been erased from your mind. I warned you, long ago. There are ways and means—hypnotic techniques . . ."

Aubretia stroked her lips thoughtfully. "Nothing you say makes sense," she murmured. "When did I know you, and where?"

"In Lon, about nine months ago. When you were Press Policy Officer in the Department of the Written Word."

"No." Aubretia shook her head slowly. "I never knew an albino. On the other hand, your name has a faintly familiar sound. Aquilegia." She repeated the name two or three times, as if trying to pinpoint the phantom recollection that hovered in the deep shadows of her brain.

"You used to call me Quilly."

No reaction.

"Why did you come here?" Aubretia asked.

Aquilegia sighed and leaned back in her chair. "It's a long story, and I could do with a drink."

"Ambrosia?"

"Fine, thanks. I'll take it neat, Aubry."

Aubretia produced a bottle of blue gin and two glasses. They drank in silence for a few minutes, studying each other covertly: Aubretia, clean and elegant and surrounded by an intangible ara of exquisite perfume, and Aquilegia, shabby and pale and wearied, bearing the marks of strain and deprivation.

"I have a confession to make," Aquilegia said presently. "I'm not who I said I am. I'm not Aquilegia. But neither you nor anyone else could tell the difference."

"Then who are you?"

"It doesn't matter. I want you to think of me as Aquilegia. She and I are alike in every smallest detail, physically and mentally. You see, she was my parthenogenetic twin."

Aubretia pursed her lips and sipped her drink, but said nothing.

"As you know, Aubry, parthenogenetic twins are identical. I knew about you and Quilly, and I knew she always had a high opinion of you. That's why I came here."

"You keep referring to this—this 'Quilly' in the past tense."

"Because she's dead. I thought that might mean something to you."

Aubretia stood up and walked purposelessly around the room. "It doesn't mean anything to me. I don't know you and I don't know your sister. I can't understand why you came here or what I could possibly do for you."

"Then let me refresh your memory," Aquilegia said ominously.

"I am a scientist," Aquilegia explained. "I work, or rather I *worked* for the Department of Biophysics. I used to be a trusted member of a secret government research unit, but I was also a member of a subversive organization. I worked in an underground laboratory on experimental cytology. Doing what? Simple enough, obvious enough, if you stop to think about it. I was trying to create a synthetic gamete with twenty-three chromosomes.

"You see the point, don't you, Aubry? A gamete with twenty-three chromosomes is a male gamete, and you can use it to fertilize a twenty-four chromosome ovum and produce a male child. But it's not so easy. The only living cells we have to deal with are female, and in five thousand years no one has ever succeeded in getting rid of the unwanted sex chromosome.

"And then the man arrived. You remember the man, don't you, Aubry? The man they found inside the rocket that was buried in the polar ice cap. He was dead, of course; dead for more than five thousand years, but in deep freeze all that time. You ought to remember, because you were the one who tried to break the news of the man on the National

Broadcast Network. Only it didn't come off. Your news story never got any further than the memory banks in the news offices, and the Department of the Written Word canceled it within seconds. And then they took you in for interrogation and questioning, Aubry. They stripped your mind bare of all it contained and they rebuilt it to their own specifications. They had nothing against you for they realized you weren't one of the subversive group. But from you they learned about my sister. She disappeared the next day. She was passed to the Department of Mortic Revenue and she paid the tax in full.

"You're beginning to understand, aren't you, Aubry. They learned about Aquilegia from you, and they learned about me from her. I was one jump ahead. I managed to get away and I've been on the run ever since. That's why I've come here—for refuge. I need help, and because of what Aquilegia was to you, I have the right to ask your help.

"You still don't see the whole picture, do you? The man in deep freeze was the answer to the problem. I spent ten years in the secret laboratory making cytological tests on thousands and thousands of male remains, the majority no more than dehydrated skeletons. And then we found a man in a state of good preservation. He was dead, admittedly, but the whole and undecayed, with a cellular structure giving for the first time a real chance of carrying out practical work on the chromosome structure of the cell nucleus.

"We couldn't bring the man back to life. We couldn't even bring a single cell back to life. But chromosomes aren't living things; they are complex molecules arranged in patterns on the cell nucleus, and they operate by biochemical mechanisms. What we could do, by precision microsurgery, was to transfer the chromosomes from a dead male cell to a living female cell. In that way we hoped to create a synthetic male gamete.

"Don't you see how, Aubry? Here you are, living in a stable society, believing that man was obliterated by nature as an unnecessary complication and was replaced by partheno-genesis. Then why should the government carry out secret experiments to recreate man? I'll tell you why; because it's all a lie. There is no such thing as natural parthenogenesis, and man didn't disappear naturally; he was destroyed. Our society is founded on that lie. We are creatures of sex living by force and unnaturally in a sexless society. We've adapted ourselves, by government edict, and by necessity. That's what the general adaptation syndrome is. We've diverted the sex instinct into other channels so that we can still achieve a sat-isfactory emotional outlet. But there's one big difference, Au-bry. The government tries to tell us it's normal, but in fact it's abnormal. We've become a race of Lesbians.

"You've never thought about it in that way, have you, Aubry? You don't even know what a Lesbian is. You're one, and I'm one, and you accept it as normal, because govern-mental policy has made it normal. It's all part of the pattern, the long-term pattern. Preserve the here-and-now at whatever cost, whatever perversion. Canalize the emotions, pervert the irrepressible natural instincts, and keep the women of the human race quiet and relatively happy. Build a stable so-cial structure on that foundation and control it rigidly by ruth-less laws of life and death. Enforce induced parthenogenesis and compulsory euthanasia as the fundamentals of modern economics; but all the time experiment and experiment to produce a male gamete and create a living male being to re-solve the inevitable result of thousands of years of partheno-genesis. Do you know what that result will be, Aubry. Do you know what will happen if the human race continues to sur-vive by artificial division of the female cells? The result will be a world of robots, assembly line creatures all alike, cast in a limited number of patterns, and working blindly under the dictates of an impersonal governing authority.

"Yes, Aubry, I said impersonal. You don't know why, and

yet you have worked for a government department. What do you know of the government? Not the officials and the administrators, but the real controlling authority which determines policy in all spheres of life. Have you ever met a true member of the government in this country, or in any other? Do you know who or what it is that governs our destinies? You look surprised, and you won't believe what I'm going to tell you, but it's true. . . .

"Don't look so anxious, Aubry. I'm not going to shock you or frighten you. All I'm going to do is tell you something you don't know, something no one knows, apart from the few members of my own circle, who are regarded as subversive. You see, we believe in truth for its own sake, just as Aquilegia did. We hold that perversion is evil, whatever the motive might be, and that the modern structure of society, based as it is on statistical birth and murder and on a homosexual morality, is wrong and corrupt throughout. And above all we object to the government of human beings by a . . ."

"By a what?" Aubretia asked.

Aquilegia (or her parthenogenetic double) remained silent for some time. Her eyes, though pale and pink, seemed to have acquired an intense burning quality that made Aubretia feel uncomfortable. Indeed, the whole trend of the near-monologue had been disquieting in the extreme, and she was not at all sure that her unkempt visitor might not be insane. Nevertheless, she was faintly aware of an undercurrent of response in her own subconscious mind, an inaudible harmonic that resonated occasionally when certain things were mentioned. The man, for instance. A fiction, obviously. Men were extinct, and it was fantastic in the extreme to allege that there was in existence a secret government laboratory containing the bodies of many men, dry and dessicated, on which experiments were being carried out to reverse the very course of nature itself. But somewhere deep within the darkness of her mind, a pallid phantom image floated hazily, the image of a white hard-boned creature of ungainly angles and unexpected hair, lying on an operating table. She could-not pinpoint the image, for it was too nebulous to stimulate a definite memory train, and she attributed it to the unsettling effect of Aquilegia's discourse.

"I think," Aquilegia finally said, slowly, "that I've said enough for the present. Quilly tried to break you in, once upon a time. But since then they've been at work on your mind and there's a limit to what you can absorb."

Aubretia leaned forward earnestly. "Please tell me," she said urgently, "about the government."

Aquilegia shook her head slowly. "Enough is enough. Let me stay here tonight and perhaps tomorrow I'll tell you some more."

"You can stay provided you tell me now."

"Well, just a brief clue, perhaps. Why do you suppose society is organized on an inhuman statistical basis, on a basis of applied mathematics? What type of government would re-gard human beings as integers in a vast complex equation? What kind of governing authority would regard individuals as units of productivity and scale their life according to their productive capacity?"

Aubretia shrugged her shoulders helplessly.

"I'll tell you," Aquilegia murmured quietly. "We are gov-erned by a machine—an electronic brain, a computor contain-ing more than ten billion digital counting units, with memory banks and integrating networks. In every way it is more effi-cient than the human brain. It can solve long-term problems of social organization and stability, but it has no soul."

"Where is this . . . this brain?" Aubretia asked.

"Everywhere. It has cellular units in every country of the world, and all the cells are linked together into a vast world brain. The brain is guarded by a small force of trained tech-nicians who feed it with statistical information concerning every conceivable aspect of human existence. And with that information the brain plans the future development of society. It is soulless and infallible; and it is secret. Even to know about it can be fatal. That is why I am a fugitive and why you, too, Aubry, may become a fugitive before very long, in spite of their hypnotic brainwashing treatment. You recognize the truth of what I am saying, don't you, Aubry."

"Yes. At least I think I do . . . some of it."

"The master brain is the supreme authority, and its computations form the basis of law and conduct, of life and death. Very few of us know the truth. The great majority of women in the world live their lives in organized peace and harmony, never enquiring beyond the erotic boundary of their own sex hormones, and accepting the mortic laws without question."

"Your party," said Aubretia. "What is its purpose?"

"We have no party. We are a few individuals who are not amenable to hypnotic techniques. We are the freethinkers of the world. We have no aim other than to spread the truth and destroy evil and perversion and corruption."

"Even if it means creating unhappiness and discontent?"

Aquilegia smiled grimly. "The truth is more important than happiness and contentment. Morality is more vital than peace and stability based on lies and Lesbianism."

Aubretia frowned in mild bewilderment. "But what kind of morality are you talking about? Five thousand years ago there were men in the world, and morality was a matter of emotional balance between men and women at a time when there was no such thing as parthenogenesis. Now we have only women and universal parthenogenesis. You can't expect the same kind of morality."

"That's the master brain talking," said Aquilegia, twisting her lips cynically. "It might be true if the evolutionary doctrine were true, that man had been eliminated as an unnecessary eugenic complication. But men destroyed himself, and artificial parthenogenesis had to come, otherwise the entire human race would have died out in one generation."

"We were talking about morality."

"It hasn't really changed in five thousand years; it has altered, and only superficially. True morality is based on the concept of two sexes. The moment you erase one of them you set up unbalance and conflict That is natural."

"I'll grant that for a moment "

"But there is *no* unbalance or conflict in the contemporary world. Not on the surface "

"So?"

"It has been resolved by the master brain in terms of homosexuality, coupled with a rigid mortic law structure."

"But isn't that better than what you call unbalance and conflict?"

Aquilegia shook her head fiercely "Not when it involves a living lie and the propagation of perversion as the right and normal thing."

Aubretia sighed, then yawned delicately "I'm afraid it's rather too deep for me, or perhaps you're trying to tell me too much in one night Let's sleep on it I have a friend, but she's out of town for two or three days, so you can stay here in the meantime. But I can only repeat that I don't remember you, or rather your parthenogenetic twin sister, Aquilegia. All that you've told me is strange and weird, and I don't know if I believe it or not."

"Given time I can convince you," said Aquilegia

In the early morning, when the sky was gray, presaging dawn, Aubretia moved silently out of her bed and dialed a number on the videophone A hard female face glared pinkly at her from the monitor screen.

"Hello," she whispered "Police headquarters. Please come right away. There's a woman in my apartment, an ex-government scientist and a member of a subversive group. She is hiding from the Department of Mortic Revenue."

The pink face remained expressionless. "Stay where you are. We shall be there within the minute."

Aubretia switched off the videophone with a sigh of relief.

PART TWO

THE MONKEY

VI

THEY kept the monkey for two years, during which time they injected some two gallons of estrogen derivative into it. Then they killed it and cut it open. Rinehart came into the laboratory to watch. He was a small shrunken man with a bristling black beard and dark birdlike eyes that gleamed restlessly. The monkey was small and brown, of the Rhesus type, with sleek fur and beady eyes glazed in death.

Slade removed the ovaries, waxed them, made microtome sections, stained them, then passed the finished slides to Gorste. He slipped them under the microscope and focused the binocular eyepiece.

"Hopeful," he said presently.

"Any sign of follicular tissue?" That was Rinehart.

"No."

"Or degeneration of the active surface?"

"I never saw a monkey with finer ovaries."

"Try the transverse sections."

Gorste changed slides. The pattern of the cells was clean and crisp, and regular as a honeycomb. He adjusted the light minutely and made a measurement with a luminance meter.

"Refractive index about normal," he said. "No sign of morbid granulation."

"And no sign of fertility."

"None whatever."

Gorste glanced briefly at Rinehart. His lips were moist where he had recently licked them, and his eyes were hard and glittering with a suppressed inner fervor. Then Gorste caught Slade's eye; the expression of the other man's face did not change, but he winked laconically

"How long will it take to prepare a complete analysis?" Rinehart asked.

Gorste considered for a moment. "About three weeks, perhaps four. There are six other monkeys and a large number of biochemical tests to be made."

"Try to hurry it up, Gorste. The board keep pressing me for results."

"I wonder if they realize the problems involved."

"They don't have to. They pay our salaries. All they are interested in is results."

"Well, results don't grow on a tree."

Rinehart pouted. "You don't have to adopt that tone with me, Gorste. I'm aware of the difficulties"

"I'm not adopting any tone," Gorste stated bluntly "At the same time I don't care to have my department criticized and hustled by a bunch of businessmen who wouldn't know a chromosome from the back end of an elephant We'll get results, but it will take time. These things can't be rushed."

Rinehart waved one hand excitedly. "Nobody is criticizing you, Gorste. The board are most satisfied with the progress you have made, and they fully realize that this job is a long-term project." He lowered his voice and leaned forward a little obsequiously. "All I'm asking is that we should have a comprehensive report to submit as soon as possible."

Gorste nodded without speaking. Rinehart paused uncertainly, smoothing the palms of his hands down his shoddy black coat. Then, wagging his head vigorously as if renouncing any responsibility for the idiosyncracies of his directors or the aggressive stubbornness of his biological research staff, he walked swiftly from the laboratory. Slade pulled a packet of cigarettes from his pocket, and the two men lit up in silence.

"Funny old codger," Slade murmured eventually, grinning faintly.

Gorste inhaled deeply and blew an abortive smoke ring. He gripped the cigarette tightly to suppress the slight trembling of his fingers. "He's a fusspot," he pronounced without emotion. "He's scared to death of the board."

"He comes into contact with them. We don't."

Gorste picked up the tail of the dead monkey and allowed it to flop back on to the dissecting board. It was already showing signs of stiffening.

"I'm damned if I can see what use this research is going to be commercially," he said. "It must have cost hundreds of thousands of dollars already."

"True."

"How can you exploit sterility as a commercial proposition?"

Slade shrugged his shoulders; his pale blue eyes were cynical. "Some people have made a fortune out of contraceptives, so why not Biochemix Incorporated?"

Gorste curled his lips doubtfully. "I'm not sure. It's going to take a great deal of hard selling to persuade women to buy an estrogen derivative injection. There are easier ways, you know."

"Yes, but how reliable?"

Gorste turned back to the microscope and inspected two more slides. They were perfect. After two years of systematic injection calculated to paralyze the normal fertility of the female monkey's reproductive system, the ovaries were abundantly healthy—but sterile. There was no discernible indication of the normal physiological cycle of ovum production. The estrogen derivative had done its job with silent efficiency.

Gorste extinguished his cigarette and pushed the microscope to the back of the bench. "By the time I've dissected and examined all of the test monkeys, I'll be dreaming about ovaries," he said sourly.

Slade twisted his mouth into a faint grin. "Coming from you, Gorste, that's funny." Then, apologetically: "That wasn't meant in any unpleasant way."

"I know what you mean, Slade."

"Have you told Anne yet?"

Gorste shook his head slowly. "I thought it would be better to wait for a while, until after this research is finished. By then I should know for certain. Tests of that kind take some time, several weeks."

Slade smiled sardonically. "I can't help feeling it's a case of physician heal thyself; only in reverse, if you see what I mean."

"Yes," said Gorste solemnly, "I do see what you mean."

The doctor had been skeptical at first, with the mildly benevolent skepticism of the medical profession. He had sat behind his old-fashioned desk in his brown and gray surgery and had listened carefully to Gorste's reasoned explanation of his fears. Gorste was sitting on a straight-backed hide chair, uncomfortably poised and slightly uneasy in manner, but his voice was calmly methodical and almost impersonal in tone.

The doctor, whose round pink face seemed to hang from his thick brown hair like a tropical fruit, was holding a silver propelling pencil like a dart, and kept making jabbing motions towards the desk top without ever making actual contact. The habit was irritating, Gorste thought, but harmless; it distracted his mind from the logical train of thought he was pursuing, so that he stopped talking prematurely.

"Interesting," said the doctor immediately. His voice was keen and incisive, like the edge of a lancet. "Of course there have been cases of that type, but they are less common than might be supposed. Only recently the A.M.J. published a survey of . . ."

"I saw it," Gorste interrupted. "As a biochemist I naturally try to keep abreast of current medical research."

"Of course. Then you are familiar with the statistics."

"Yes, doctor. But *I'm* not a statistic."

The doctor flicked his silver pencil towards the desk, misjudged the distance and broke the point. Gorste felt gratified. The doctor twisted the pencil until a new point protruded, then resumed his target practice.

"This accident you mentioned," he said. "Can you supply a little more detail?"

"It happened about eighteen months ago," Gorste explained. "At that time I was working in a nuclear research establishment under the Department of Supply. My particular job was to investigate the effect of hard radiation—gamma radiation, for instance—on living animals. It's a subject we know all too little about. One of the objects of the research program was to determine the extent to which ambient gamma radiation in the atmosphere might act as a carcinogenic factor."

"You were engaged in cancer research?"

"Not exactly, but it came into the sphere of our investigations. We used radioactive materials and in some cases dangerous uranium isotopes in our tests on animals. The isotopes are normally stored in heavy lead containers, and are generally handled by remote control equipment known as a robot hand."

The doctor nodded briskly and put his silver pencil in his pocket.

"Well, the accident just . . . happened. It wasn't really

an 'accident' at all. You see, doctor, one of my colleagues tried to kill me. He was a man called Drewin and there had been some misunderstanding about his wife. It was before I was married, of course.

The doctor leaned forward abruptly, a new alertness gleaming in his eyes. "You mean that you were having an affair with this Drewin's wife?"

"It wasn't quite like that; it was what you might call a passing infatuation. It lasted about a month. Then Drewin committed suicide."

"I see; so the infatuation came to a sudden end."

"Naturally."

"You say he tried to kill you."

Gorste nodded slowly. "I didn't find out until five weeks later. I was making a Geiger test on a dead animal on my bench in the laboratory, and the needle of the Geiger counter nearly wrapped itself round the stop. There seemed to be a devil of a lot of radioactivity around and it wasn't all coming from the specimen. Well, I tracked it down."

Gorste paused, drawing in his lips bitterly. "You may find it difficult to believe, doctor, but this man Drewin had removed a container of uranium isotope from its lead case and had fixed it under my bench. I found the case hidden in a cardboard box under his bench. That was how I knew who had been responsible."

Breathing heavily, the doctor retrieved his silver pencil from his pocket and held it poised over the desk. "That would kill you, of course."

"In time. The thing was cleated to the underside of the bench top, near the front. Every day for God knows how many weeks I was being bombarded by hard nuclear radiation. In fact, I developed radiation poisoning."

"Who treated you for it?"

"Nobody. I kept it to myself."

The doctor placed his pencil carefully on the desk, then

stood up and paced the floor, glancing obliquely at Gorste. His eyes were thoughtful, eyebrows slightly raised.

"Why?" he demanded.

"Well," said Gorste, shrugging vaguely, "Drewin had gassed himself. There was no good-bye note, or if there was his wife had destroyed it. I wasn't implicated, and the inquest returned the usual verdict about the balance of the mind being disturbed, and so on. If I'd reported the business of the uranium isotope—if I'd even sought medical aid—the whole story might have come out. For the sake of Drewin's wife, and Drewin himself, dead though he was, I thought it best to say nothing."

"You weren't thinking of yourself, of course."

"I had nothing to lose, doctor."

The doctor said nothing for a moment. He returned to his desk and sat down heavily, then picked up the pencil and pointed it accusingly at Gorste.

He said: "About the uranium. How far were you from it when working normally at the bench?"

"Six inches to twelve inches."

"What was the bench made of?"

"Wood with a plastic surface. It wouldn't stop any kind of nuclear radiation."

"And how high was the bench?"

"About three feet, perhaps a little less."

The doctor's eyes scanned the seated length of Gorste's slender body, finally settling on his abdomen. "The stomach and pelvic area," he stated. "Regions of maximum radioactive contamination."

"When you come to examine me," Gorste said, "you'll find traces of a radiation burn just here." He placed one hand over the lower part of his abdomen.

"And you think that as a result of this, this intensive exposure to nuclear radiation, you have become sterile."

"I'm absolutely certain of it."

The doctor stroked his chin thoughtfuly. "How long have you been married, Mr. Gorste?"

"About a year, just a little more. We had our first anniversary three weeks ago."

"Well," said the doctor heavily, with an air of decision, "it is by no means abnormal for a woman to fail to achieve pregacy during the first year of marriage. Sometimes it may last for two years, or three, or more. There are many cases where a perfectly fertile man and woman are incapable of having a child at all, and for no good reason that doctors can discover."

Gorste smiled grimly, as if he knew about doctors and didn't like what he knew. "My case is different. For one thing I know my wife is fertile. During her first marriage she was pregnant twice, but on each occasion there was a miscarriage. So the fault must lie with myself. In view of the radioactive accident I mentioned I think it's fairly obvious that I have what you might call an advanced case of induced sterility."

"Very well," said the doctor, conceding the point. "I'll have a laboratory test made. For the moment I propose to make a preliminary examination. It is quite probable that you may be right."

After the examination, when Gorste was preparing to go, the doctor said: "About Drewin's wife. What happened to her after her husband killed himself?"

Gorste hesitated a moment, buttoning his overcoat with precision movements of his delicate fingers. He moved towards the door, not looking at the doctor.

"I married her," he said, then made his exit.

After he had placed the remains of the Rhesus monkey in the laboratory refrigerator, Gorste removed his white overall and went into the washroom to freshen up for his journey home. Slade was in there, and Ingram. From the broad grin on Slade's face and the jolly tone of Ingram's voice, Gorste deduced that Ingram was reciting one of his improper jokes.

"And there in the bedroom was a hammock," Ingram was saying, "and he said what's the big idea and she said I thought you liked doing things the hard way."

Slade's guffaw reverberated hollowly from the tiled walls of the washroom. The point had been made and the joke was over and Slade was performing the complex lung-voice ritual known as laughter, and Ingram's long thin face was beaming with radiant smugness. Gorste turned on the taps and washed his hands carefully, anxious to remove the odor of formaldehyde from his fingers. From the corner of his eye he saw Ingram approaching.

"Congratulations," came Ingram's smooth voice. "I understand the world's going to be a much brighter place any time at all, thanks to you, Gorste."

"Mm?" Gorste murmured, turning his head slightly.

"This new contraceptive you've developed."

Gorste grimaced mentally. "I wish you wouldn't refer to my work in that way, Ingram. My job is biochemical research, and the commercial applications are none of my business."

"But it's *my* business," said Ingram pleasantly. Gorste recalled that the other man was a member of the sales promotion staff of the company. He had been a representative, out on the road, and his appointment to a staff job in the sales office was a fairly recent event. He eyed Ingram with a certain veiled hostility: he looked every inch the salesman: smooth, suave, affable, talkative, and never at a loss for a good story or anecdote.

"You're too sensitive," Ingram went on. "The manufacture and distribution of contraceptives is one of the major industries of our society. You'd be surprised if you realized the ramifications. Birth control is related to population level, and that in turn affects the economics of modern life."

Gorste grunted noncommittaly, wishing Ingram were several light-years away.

"Do you realize," Ingram persisted, "that what you are doing now might alter the whole structure of society as we know it. This estro thing you've developed . . ."

"Estrogen derivative."

"That's what I said. Do you realize, Gorste, that . . ."

"I realize it's twenty-five past six," Gorste said shortly, "and that I should have been halfway home by now."

Ingram chuckled synthetically. "Of course. I forgot you were a married man. I'll take it up with you some other time."

Gorste turned to go, but Ingram's voice came provocatively over his shoulder. "Did you hear about the man who liked doing things the hard way? Used to cut the grass with a pair of nail scissors and when he got married insisted on picking up the confetti off the carpet with a pin . . ."

"I'm sorry," said Gorste, glancing at his wrist watch. "I really do have to go."

When Gorste had left, Slade said to Ingram: "You ought to be more careful, Ingram. Never talk about sterility or contraceptives to Gorste."

Ingram's eyes registered genuine surprise. "But that's his job."

"I know, but there's something else that alters the picture. You see, Ingram, Gorste is sterile."

For an instant Ingram's narrow face was solemn and uncomprehending, then abruptly he burst into laughter. He nudged Slade in the ribs. "That's rich! Gosh, I must remember that! The inventor of mass sterility is sterile!"

He kept on laughing in his artificial manner until Slade became embarrassed. He excused himself and left the room.

VII

Home was a house, Gorste was thinking, *but not an empty house. There must be furniture and possessions and some of*

*the possessions had to be trivial, like an empty tooth paste
tube or an ash tray garnished with cigarette stubs—symbols
of human occupation. And there had to be a clock, a reliable clock, for the routine of any home was largely actuated
by the time of day. And for a married man there had to be a
wife.*

From where he was sitting in his home Gorste could see
both the clock and his wife; both were attractive in a superficial way. The clock, for instance, was a rectangle in chrome
and white, with green triangles in place of figures, and the
hands were slender and black, with a pale strip of luminous
matter painted on them (that would be a compound containing radioactive thorium, he recalls with a faint sense of
irony). The wife was smooth and rounded and auburn-
haired, not less than thirty and looking her age, but with a
poised, almost deliberate, air of maturity. Her eyes were
brown and a little narrow, but her face was pleasant enough
and her lips were invitingly bowed. She dressed well. The
dark crimson dress she wore made her look vaguely movie-like
to Gorste's eyes, like a portion of a still from a technicolor
film. But perhaps that's because she *was* a still, a motionless
image in a kind of deep freeze, with static eyes fixed on the
tiny moving shapes of the television screen.

Occasionally Gorste glanced perfunctorily at the television
set. A panel game of some kind, one of the many. Four ex-
perts guessed some unimportant triviality to the accompani-
ment of enthusiastic applause from an unseen studio audience. Disseminated to the nation by the miracle of radio
transmission, it was fascinating if you felt in the mood, but
Gorste didn't feel in the mood.

The radioactive hand of the clock advanced round the dial
with the slowness of eternity, and had been doing so for the
past two hours. During that time the only sound in the room
had been the synthetic voice of the television receiver. Not
quite accurate: there had been an occasion when Gorste vol-

unteered to make coffee and Anne nodded briefly, and the coffee was made and consumed with a murmured thanks. *Robots Incorporated,* Gorste thought, *but in twenty minutes television would be finished and the human mind would reassert its control over the human brain, and the hypnotic seizure of human consciousness by electronic shadows would cease for another day. Life would return to normal at bedtime.*

Life and night and bed had become synonymous, and the business of human relationships became compressed into the twilight fringe between the end of television and the beginning of sleep. Meanwhile Gorste looked at Anne and at the clock, and he counted off the minutes to the end of this modern electronic narcotic.

Looking at Anne was by no means a penance. There was a time when it had been a distinct pleasure, before the death of Drewin, before the slow concretion of routine marriage relationships, before life had become complicated by matters of fertility and sterility. It was still a pleasure, but with reservations. She was attractive enough within her own terms of reference, and her body still held the eternal promise of her sex, unconditionally. But a body wasn't everything; sometimes a brain was an asset, and sometimes, to a scientist with an academic turn of mind, the occasional sluggish turning of intelligence could be a flashing jewel in the gloom of psychic noncommunication.

Or am I being smug? Gorste asked himself. *Am I judging Anne too harshly, by standards far removed from the level of normal life? Am I expecting too much from a stolen woman? Or, getting down to fundamentals, are we really incompatible, and did I make the supreme mistake in taking her as my wife? What in the long run is the basic attraction? A matter of biological chemistry, of hormones and discreet physiology, or a matter of psychological compulsion, of mother fixation or image transference? Why do I love her,*

*or more simply, do I love her? And, in framing such a ques-
tion, am I not confessing that I do not love her?*

The panel game was nearing its end. Somebody had won
eight thousand dollars and the studio audience was applaud-
ing wildly, and presently the commercials will come on and
smooth young men and women will talk about detergents and
gasoline and cider and margarine. And Anne will withdraw
slowly from the world of the small screen and condense, as it
were, into a living human in the here and now. Time is short
for private thought: soon must come the small talk and the
phrases of affection crystallizing into the inevitable pseudo-
romantic atmosphere of bedtime.

But why pseudo? And pseudo to whom? What in the last
analysis was romance, practical functioning romance of the
kind that welded married people into an integral bisexual
unit? To what extent was romance a projection of sexual as-
piration? Or was that begging the question: was sex, after all,
the common denominator of all male-female relationships,
and was the fumbling confusion of individual relationships a
synthesis of that basic instinct, sublimated and distorted into
planes of feeling and emotion that have no fundamental objective reality?

Gorste was in an analytical mood, and for the moment his
wife is as distant and impersonal as the rectangular clock
over the fireplace. But soon she will unfreeze into warmth
and motion and he would respond as always, in accordance
with the established pattern of behavior. He would take over
where the TV left off.

Supposing I told her I am sterile, he thought. How would
she react? She wants a child, the child that Drewin was
never able to give her. Would she retreat into herself, seal-
ing her emotions and assuming a static frigidity, or would she
be sympathetic? It was Drewin's fault, after all, but one
could hardly mention that. And how important was sterility,
anyway? If the basis of romantic feeling between two indi-

viduals was sexual, as it must be, then how could the fact of sterility affect it or modify it in any way. Sterility as such was a long-term physiological factor. It didn't influence the short-term personal relationship between a man and a woman. It was, in fact, a kind of contraceptive, and as such was fourth dimensional in effect, being a function of time. Each act of amorous relationship was in itself unaffected by the fact of sterility, but the poison accumulates in the months that follow, in the absence of conception and pregnancy. To a man, thinks Gorste, *it might not matter; but to a woman it might be all important.*

The panel game was ended, and the commercials were under way. Anne stirred, returned to life. She turned and smiled faintly at her husband.

"Sandra Graham was good wasn't she, darling? And Cheryl Dawn, too. The way they answered that question about the theodolite. I nearly screamed."

I didn't notice it, Gorste told himself. *I didn't notice anything. The scream, if ever it came near to existence, was stillborn. Sterile reaction. Electronic emotion.*

"Kiss me," said Anne.

Gorste moved over to her chair and kissed her.

"Again," she said.

He complied. *In a moment,* he thought, *her fingers will take my hand and place it over her breast, and she will say let's go to bed, and the opening gambit will begin in the orthodox way, and I will make my move and she will make hers, and presently we shall go to bed because we want to and not because we have to, for that's the way it is when television is finished.*

The detergent had given way to a gasoline, and in a moment Anne's fingers closed around Gorste's hand and moved it downwards towards her breast.

Gorste said nothing about his sterile condition that night.

It was partly lack of courage, and partly lack of opportunity, for Anne adhered strictly to the rules of romantic progression, almost systematically, Gorste told himself, and there was not a spare instant for any kind of talk outside the normal established run of dialogue. And even the dialogue faded into silence as the demands of the body overruled the needs of the mind. And when the body finally relinquished its obsessive requisition of thought and feeling and physical response, there was nothing left, and the mind, in the ensuing flowing blankneses, sank exquisitely into unconsciousness. That's how it always had been, and presumably that's how it always would be. There was no room for truth and confession and serious talk about the future.

Anne was still asleep when Gorste left for the laboratory the next morning. He sensed a certain regret and frustration in his failure to broach the subject of steriliy to his wife, although, he told himself consolingly, it wasn't so much a failure as an absence of conversational opening. There was always tomorrow, and tomorrow always seemed to be a better day than today for performing unpleasant duties. There might be time this evening, perhaps. After television, of course.

He met Rinehart in the corridor leading to the laboratory. Rinehart made cryptic motions at him with both hands, then whisked him into his office.

"Sit down, Gorste."

Gorste sat down on a steel tube and canvas chair. Rinehart hovered around him like a venturous moth round a flame.

"The board is pressing things a little," Rinehart said in a tentative manner. An understatement, Gorste thought. "Naturally the commercial side of things requires a great deal of planning. To market a product successfully may need a year or more of advance thinking and discussion at different levels.

And with a product of this type there is so much more to be considered . . ."

"A product of what type?"

Quick shuffling of patent leather shoes. "A commercial form of estrogen derivative, of course. Naturally"—a swift smile—"the product cannot be marketed in the same way as one would promote a new brand of toothpaste, or a breakfast cereal. The whole problem is much more complex, and there will have to be very many conferences with the advertising agency and the packaging department and the various other interests concerned. And, even more important, there must of necessity be close liaison with the government, in particular with the Ministry of Health."

"Agreed; so . . ?"

"Well, obviously, preparations begin at an early date."

"How early?"

"Today . . . this afternoon."

Gorste touched his ear pensively but said nothing.

"The managing director is calling a planning and sales promotion meeting after lunch. The advertising account executive will be there. You will be there, too."

"Me?"

"The managing director specifically asked for you."

"Nice of her. Does she realize this thing is as yet no more than a series of tests on monkeys? We haven't even begun to think of tests on human beings."

Rinehart waved his hands in an abortive circle. "That will come in time. First results are promising—more than promising. Even on the basis of monkey tests we can begin to sketch out the shape of a sales promotion campaign."

Gorste snorted mildly.

"You must remember," Rinehart continued, "that all of us are part of a commercial organization, an organization that is in business for one purpose only—to make a profit. Your laboratory is part of the profit-making mechanism."

"I realize that," Gorste said patiently. "All I ask is that we should be allowed to walk before we are forced to run. Let's be logical, Rinehart. How can E. J. Wasserman even think in terms of sales promotion at this stage, when we are still dissecting monkeys?"

Rinehart beamed. "Because E. J. has the utmost faith and confidence in you and your research team, and because these things have to be planned many, many months in advance."

"All right," Gorste conceded reluctantly. "I'll be there. But I don't like it. I don't like it at all."

Rinehart's hand flicked like a snake's tongue towards Gorste's shoulder and patted it fraternally. "I knew I could rely on you, Gorste," he murmured with mock affability, and then he was moving away along the corridor, poised stiffly on the quick short movements of his stubby legs.

When Gorste arrived in the conference room the long table was already full. E. J. Wasserman sat at the head, looking cool and confident, defying the half century of years that had overpowered her youth and beauty. Sometimes Gorste thought it strange that a woman (an attractive enough woman when you looked at her from the right angle in the right light) should be managing director of a vast chemical combine, but there was nothing weak and effeminate about E. J. when it came to the point. It seemed logical that her husband should have died more than ten years earlier: the immovable object disintegrates in the presence of an unstoppable force.

Other directors and executives of the company lined either side of the table, talking quietly among themselves, or looking respectfully and attentively towards E. J., who was smoking a cigarette with quick masculine movements of her hands and lips.

Gorste made his way towards the empty chair alongside Rinehart. As he sat down, Rinehart glanced quickly at his wristwatch and whispered from the corner of his mouth:

"Two minutes late, Gorste. Let's hope E. J. didn't notice."

Gorste made no comment. All eyes seemed to be focused on him for a few seconds, and then E. J.'s voice cut astringently through the silence.

"Very well, gentlemen. Let us begin." She riffled a sheaf of papers without looking at them "Subject: estrogen derivative; formula: three nine two."

"Three nine three," said a man called Lowery apologetically.

E. J.'s eyes seemed to click as they swung towards Gorste. His voice broke into spontaneous sound.

"Three nine two, E. J. We shan't be ready for the three nine three dissections for several weeks."

E. J.'s eyes held his for a brief embarrassing moment. Those eyes, green and wide, possessed a certain hypnotic quality; they contrasted with the rich cream of her complexion and the bronzed auburn of her hair. It was as if E. J. had noticed him for the very first time, and the reaction modified his heartbeat.

"According to the early biophysical reports," said E. J. crisply, "it would seem that formula three nine two has the characteristics we require for a commercial product. Isn't that so, Mr. Gorste?"

Gorste attempted to resurrect the stubbornness that seemed to have died within him. "We are still in an experimental stage," he said lamely. "The indications are good, but we are still working on monkeys. It may be that . . ."

"Indications are enough," E. J. cut in brusquely. "We are here to make long-term plans on the assumption that formula three nine two or a subsequent development of it will be suitable for marketing as a commercial product in, say, a year. All I need to know at this stage is this: does formula three nine two produce sterility?"

"Yes," said Gorste.

"And will it produce sterility in a human female?"

"Yes."

"For how long?"

"About six months, I think. Perhaps a little more."

"One hundred per cent sterility?"

"Yes."

E. J. nodded in satisfaction. For a woman of fifty, Gorste thought, she wasn't at all bad. Too positive in manner, perhaps, but still feminine. It seemed strange to hear a woman discussing sterility so candidly and impersonally.

"About the administration," E. J. said, questioningly.

Gorste considered for a moment, pouting. "At the moment, hypodermic . . . intravenous, in fact. But Weyland is working on a gastric absorption type which can be taken in tablet form. We don't know yet whether it will be effective that way."

"Let's assume it will be," E. J. pronounced dogmatically. "As I see it we shall soon be able to go into full production on a sterility tablet which will make the problem of birth control and contraception obsolete. One tablet and a glass of water will provide absolute security against pregnancy for six months." A pause, while she rotated her eyes like radar antennae and focused them upon a slender baldheaded man seated halfway down the table on the opposite side from Gorste.

"Mr. Gosling," she said firmly. "The product must have a name."

Gosling shifted uncomfortably in his chair. Gorste recognized him as a member of the advertising agency handling the Biochemix Incorporated account. He was probably the account executive, to judge by his uneasiness.

"We've worked hard on it, E. J.," Gosling stated. "A product of this type must have a dignified name, one which suggests its function yet at the same time is in no way salacious, or capable of misinterpretation, either deliberately or otherwise. A strong name, easy to remember, and simple. Above all

—a selling name. The kind of name that people wouldn't feel ashamed to ask for in a shop."

"Well?"

"It must also be the kind of name which can be used in advertising without descriptive copy. The one word by itself must tell the whole story. Only in that way would any kind of consumer advertising be ethically permissible."

"Agreed. Have you thought of a name?"

Gosling hesitated, licking his lips briefly. "Yes, E. J. It's a good name. We've vetted it from every angle. It will sell. It doesn't offend in any way. It can be used for single-word advertising."

"Yes . . . ?"

"Sterilin."

E. J. paused, eyeing Gosling thoughtfully. "Sterilin," she murmured slowly, as if savoring the feel of the word on her tongue. "Sterilin." She became brisk in manner. "That's a good name, Mr. Gosling. Excellent. Your agency has done a good job."

Gosling brightened perceptibly. Self-assurance dawned in his eyes. He shrugged and smiled. "Naturally we put in a great deal of work on it, E. J. More than two hundred names, and we eliminated all but one. We even drew up a rough logotype."

He fumbled beneath his chair and produced a briefcase from which he extracted a rectangle of cardboard covered by a sheet of flimsy paper. He passed it across the table to E. J. She lifted the flimsy and studied the neat flowing lettering painted on the card.

"Not bad," she observed. "Too modern and streamlined if anything."

Gosling coughed drily. "We tried to make it look a little . . . well, what you might call racy. Zest, youthfulness, energy. After all, birth control is only one half of the sales story. Sterilin has a more positive selling angle: uninhibited enjoyment of the pleasures of life." He stroked his bald head, watching E. J. anxiously.

E. J. glanced towards a thick-set mustached man whom Gorste recognized as Dewer, the company's sales manager. "What do you think, Mr. Dewer?"

"Risky policy," Dewer stated briefly, moving his mustache almost imperceptibly. "Mustn't suggest such a thing in either advertising or packaging."

"We don't suggest anything," Gosling insisted. "It's a simple matter of lettering style. In the draft logotype we've adopted a gay youthful form of script. The implications are on a purely psychological level."

Dewer reached across the table for the card and studied it doubtfully. "Could be. What's the alternative?"

"Something staid and old-fashioned, something like you'd find on a bottle of family cough mixture."

Dewer returned the card to E. J. "I like it," he affirmed. "It does exactly as Gosling says. It's racy. It suggests fun. That mightn't be a bad angle for a sales campaign."

E. J. nodded, then turned her sea-green eyes towards Gorste. "The tablets," she said, "must be pleasant to take, with nothing medicinal about them. Pleasant to the taste . . invigorating. With fizz, perhaps."

"You mean an effervescent coating," said Gorste. "That could be arranged."

"And white in color to suggest purity."

Gosling shook his head. "I would suggest red. It has warmth; it creates a suitable atmosphere."

E. J. regarded him sternly. "Mr. Gosling, we are not marketing an aphrodisiac. Sterilin is to be a prestige product, and we don't need to be too racy. I still think the logotype is suggestive in the wrong way. It needs restraint. The script should be a thinner line, and more upright."

"If you say so, E. J."

"But I like the name. It is most suitable. Make a note of it, Dewer. 'Sterilin—for modern feminine hygiene.' "

"Hygiene?" 'Dewer queried.

"It can hardly be described in any other way without making offensive implications."

"Why describe it at all, E. J.?" said Gosling. "The word Sterilin is enough. It arouses curiosity and it implies its purpose. Any further information can be obtained at the point of sale."

"Not in the first instance. The product has to be established. It has to be forced onto the market. The public has to be told about it through the usual advertising media."

"Then something simple . . . enigmatic. How about: 'Secure for Six Months—Sterilin. Ask at your local druggist'?"

"On the beam," Dewer remarked with enthusiasm. "That would start them asking."

"It has to be angled at women," E. J. said.

"Not necessarily. Men have a fifty per cent interest in this product."

"But women will use it."

Gosling said: "We could have an introductory headline. For women only."

"That would make the men read it," said Dewer.

"And the women, too. All of them. There's a clannishness about women, a kind of invisible freemasonry."

"I hadn't noticed it," E. J. remarked sardonically. "But I think Gosling is right. 'For women only: Security for Six Months—Sterilin—Ask at your local druggist.' I like that. What about you, Dewer?"

"Not bad at all; good, in fact."

"Very well. We have the outline of a possible advertising campaign. It strikes the right note and will stimulate curiosity. Provided the product lives up to its promise we shall have a best seller."

E. J. looked around the table with a gleam of subdued

satisfaction in her green eyes. She paused as she looked at
Gorste, and he thought he could detect something provoca-
tive in the way she regarded him. It was not an unpleasant
feeling, and, in fact, he found it vaguely flattering. An instant
later her eyes moved on, leaving him suddenly desolated.

"Packaging," E. J. pronounced solemnly. Her gaze settled
on a slender bleached cadaver of a man leaning mournfully
over a cardboard folder fat with papers.

"Pettifer," she said. "What have you done about it?"

Pettifer stroked the polished table top with spidery fingers.
"Very little, E. J. After all, what have we got to package at
this stage? A dead monkey or two."

E. J.'s lips tightened into a thin ruby line, then relaxed
slowly. "You're being obstructive, Pettifer. We are looking
ahead, thinking in terms of a tablet product which has to be
packaged attractively, discreetly and in a distinctive way."

"I know, E. J.," said Pettifer wanly. "I've had several ses-
sions with the advertising agency on the subject." He hooked
a bony thumb towards Gosling. "With Mr. Gosling in particular."

"We have a number of draft packagings," Gosling put in,
fumbling in his brief case. "Naturally it all depends on the
kind of tablet: the shape and size and color." He placed a
number of tubular containers wrought in glass and plastics
of various colors on the table, then a handful of folded cardboard boxes resembling toothpaste tubes. E. J. surveyed them
all critically.

"Antiquated," she said. "The day of the cardboard container is finished. As I see it the container for Sterilin must be
ultra-modern, imaginative, self-dispensing, automatic. Above
all, it must be feminine."

Gosling toyed with a pink tube. "These can be adapted.
They're purely basic. The logotype can be transfer printed
on to the case."

"I don't want a tube of aspirins," E. J. stated dogmatically. "I don't want a tube of anything. A tube is the wrong shape. It's masculine. I want something feminine."

Gorste, intrigued by E. J.'s line of attack, found himself trying to think of a typical feminine shape, but his mind remained blank.

"A compact, for instance," E. J. went on, "a cavity that opens: pretty, perfumed, even heart-shaped and gilted. The tablets must be packed flat, side by side. See what I mean."

"Yes, E. J.," Gosling murmured. "It could be done."

"I want Sterilin to be packed like a cosmetic, an aid to feminine allure. When you get down to fundamentals that's what it will mean." Then, to Pettifer: "Do you agree?"

Pettifer nodded glumly, interlacing his skeletal fingers. "I must confess I hadn't thought of it in quite that way. I'd always regarded the estrogen derivative as a clinical product. You seem to have put the thing in a completely different light, E. J."

"A logical light, I hope, Mr. Pettifer. Sterilin is going to influence the whole moral climate of our society, of every society in the world. I have the export market in view, too. There will be no need for subterfuge. Sterilin will set women free, release them from the subconscious fear of pregnancy that has always inhibited their relationships with men. The packaging must be in tone with that concept. We have a good name. All we need now is a good package."

"You're right," Pettifer conceded reluctantly.

E. J. waved a disdainful hand at the cluster of tube and containers on the table. "Take them away, Mr. Gosling. Think again—in terms of cosmetics."

"A gilded compact," breathed Gosling incredulously.

"That's a basic proposition," said E. J. "Take it from there. No tubes or bottles or pill boxes. Something glamorous and enchanting. The package in itself should stimulate sales."

"I'll work on it, E. J.," Gosling affirmed.

E. J. paused, looking around the table once more. Again

her eyes made contact with Gorste's, and this time they
stayed with him, piercing him hypnotically with more than
a hint of friendliness. Tentatively, he held her gaze, striving
to inject a quality of admiration into his expression without
knowing why, but presently he looked down at the table,
then at his fingers which were tapping lightly and nervously
on the polished wood.

"We have gone as far as we can go in the technical sense,"
E. J. stated. "Product name and packaging are both defined. We are now waiting on the research department. Perhaps Mr. Gorste would like to give us an assessment of future
development in the light of what we have already discussed."

Gorste swallowed painfully against a dry tongue, cursing
himself for his nerves. Why should a woman like E. J. Wasserman unsettle him? She was remote, elderly (even if well
preserved), with a type of mind completely alien to his own
kind of psychology. And yet he was very conscious of her,
even though his eyes were stubbornly directed towards the
table and his fingers. His voice, when he spoke, sounded flat
and toneless in his ears; that pleased him to some extent, for
he felt that it made him sound matter-of-fact, almost laconic.

He said: "Well, E. J., it has been most interesting for me,
a what you might call 'backroom boy' of the company, to sit
in on a conference of this type and hear something of a side
of the business completely unknown to me. I . . . I must
confess that I have never thought of estrogen derivative,
formula three nine two, as a cosmetic. There is nothing
glamorous about a dead monkey or a slice of simean ovary
under a microscope. Perhaps I tend to get out of touch with
the realities of the world of industry and commerce."

He waited for a moment, pleased at the trend of his discourse, and satisfied with the dead-pan sound of his words.
Briefly he glanced up and caught E. J.'s eyes. She was still
watching him intently.

"You talk about tablets," he continued. "The fact is we

are still far from the tablet stage. The estrogen derivative, as it exists, is only effective when injected directly into the blood plasma. Weyland is experimenting with an ingestible formula, but results so far haven't been particularly encouraging. It might be completely false to assume that a tablet type of estrogen would have the same long-term effect as the plasma type. For example, it might not sustain sterility for six months at all, perhaps not even for six weeks."

"It is my experience," E. J. said quietly, "that every new drug introduced by this company started as an injection. But in nearly every case our research biochemists were able to produce an ingestible type in a palatable form." Her voice became softer, more personal. "I feel sure that Mr. Gorste and his staff will produce the kind of tablet we require for our sales campaign."

"Possibly," said Gorste "It will take time. To my mind all this talk of advertising and packaging is premature The product as such does not even exist at the present time."

"But as soon as it does exist we shall have it on the market with the minimum of delay," E. J. pointed out. "These things take time. To lose even eight weeks of selling time might mean a loss of many thousands of pounds to the company. That is why we are making our plans early."

Gorste said: "One other thing worries me: what you might call the ethics of sales promotion. I am a scientist, and I think in terms of the abstract. If what I am producing is a contraceptive, then it seems objectionable to me that the thing should be exploited as some kind of—of cosmetic."

"Don't confuse the packaging with the product," E. J. interrupted. "The object of the package is to sell, and when I referred to a cosmetic compact I was merely indicating the type and style of container I visualized for Sterilin. Many products sell on package style alone."

"With this product there is no necessity for a selling package," Gorste insisted. "If it is any good it will sell itself.

It would be unethical to promote the thing by an intensive sales campaign, or by employing underhand techniques—glamor compacts, for instance. We are still on clinical ground."

E. J.'s smile was kindly and almost condescending. "I'm afraid you are confused on fundamentals, Mr. Gorste, but for a scientist that is perhaps understandable. Sales promotion is an essential part of any industry, and in some cases it can even be more important than the product. A good promotion campaign and a good package can sell a bad product, but when you have a good product you can't go wrong. Turnover increases, profits rise, and the shareholders get bigger dividends. And dividends are the life's blood of any commercial venture."

Gorste said nothing, and his very silence registered disapproval.

"It's a subtle viewpoint," E. J. continued "One that takes a great deal of time to explain to one accustomed to thinking in the abstract. I don't propose to delay matters by dealing with it now, but later—after the conference is finished—perhaps you might like to come to my office. I'll try to present the facts of business life to you more clearly."

Gorste looked into her keen, almost eager, eyes, and nodded slowly, conscious of a strange instability in the rhythm of his heart.

"Meanwhile, Mr. Gorste, perhaps you would be kind enough to outline for us the present state of progress in the development of Sterilin."

"All right," Gorste murmured thoughtfully, struggling to keep his mind away from the hypnotic eyes of the woman across the table. "I will."

VIII

ALTHOUGH the Biochemix building was a modern structure in austere, cubic style, E. J.'s office held a dated and faintly antiquated atmosphere. It was, Gorste thought, an anachronism in the ostentatious futurist architecture of the building as a whole, but a comfortable and luxurious anachronism. The furniture was big and heavily upholstered, and the desk, in polished mahogany, had an expensive solidity that toned perfectly with the moulded ceiling and the hanging crystal chandelier. The furnishing and decor were hardly office-like at all. There was a cozy domesticity about the place, suggestive of a small drawing room. The settee, for instance, had no business in any office, and worse still, the tapestry surface bore indentations that suggested frequent use. Only the window was modern, being oblong with immense rectangular panes, but the curtains were heavy and velvety, and they were halfdrawn to occlude any excess of daylight.

Gorste, looking at E. J. in close-up, found himself fascinated, though he would have been hard put to define the exact nature of his fascination, or the specific features of the woman that exerted such undeniable magnetism She was mature, yet, despite her age, which so far as Gorste knew was in the late forties, (if not in the early fifties), her figure was slim and adequately shaped. Even her face, though bearing the wrinkles of advancing years, possessed an alertness, an innate liveliness, that suggested inherent youthfulness. She had poise. She dressed well in dark, slim-tapered clothes. Her hair was immaculate. The cosmetic on her face was skillfully applied, but not overapplied. She was obviously a woman who could afford to be efficiently and expensively groomed.

It was not without some misgivings that Gorste reported

to her office, as requested. E. J. Wasserman, whatever her sex or appearance, was the managing director of Biochemix, and at that level, sex was a matter of negligible significance. Gorste was aware of a vaguely unpleasant feeling that he had erred—sinned against the company's policy—in some indefinable way. Perhaps it had to do with his mildly implied criticism of the projected sales promotion and advertising campaign, or it could have been the lukewarm atmosphere of his attitude towards the Sterilin research program in general. He was aware of a microscopic element of guilt, of cynical disloyalty; and now, standing face to face with the woman who was his employer, a certain sense of confusion embarrassed him.

But E. J.'s smile was genuine enough, and her voice was warm and friendly.

"Please sit down, Mr. Gorste."

Gorste sat down, uncomfortably, on a padded chair. E. J. remained standing, moving around a little, glancing at him occasionally.

"It's a long time since we met in this office," said E. J.

"Yes, indeed," Gorste murmured formally, "many years, in fact."

It had been on the ocasion of his appointment as head research biochemist in the company's laboratory. Then E. J. had said to him: "We've an important program of work ahead of us, Mr. Gorste, and I believe you're the man to do it. You won't see much of me, but I'll be watching your work and I'm confident you will serve us well. And in return we shall pay you well." That was so long ago it might have been a dream, but now this was the same E. J., the same in every detail, so far as Gorste could remember, but right now just a little more intimate in manner than he might have expected.

"I realize," she said, "that a research scientist might very well be uninformed as to the commercial activities of the company for which he works." She smiled pleasantly. "By uninformed, I mean 'unaware,' in the sense of being otherwise preoccupied. Naturally you are very much concerned in your research program; perhaps so much so that it might seem as if the research side is an end in itself, is self-sustaining."

"It does seem that way at times," Gorste conceded.

"In fact, Mr. Gorste, the research laboratory is a very small part of the mechanism of Biochemix. Don't misunderstand me: small but important—extremely important. But in terms of revenue, and dividends, definitely small. Frankly, the laboratory operates at a loss, though naturally the loss is absorbed in the overall economics of the company."

"I don't follow," Gorste said stubbornly. "Nearly every product this company ever marketed began life in the lab. Without the lab there would be no products and no profits."

"Nevertheless, the lab remains nonproductive in the commercial sense. It is a service, an industrial service that is expensive but essential." E. J. crossed to the window and looked out for a moment across the massed outbuildings of the factory sloping towards the distant road. Rain fell mistily, flattening and obscuring the view. Presently, turning to Gorste, she went on: "The point I wish to make is that company policy is determined by the sales division of the company; it is based on commercial factors. For that reason it may at times seem strange, perhaps immoral, to our research staff who live in the more rarefied atmosphere of the laboratory."

Gorste noted and ignored the faint bite of sarcasm in her voice. She was silhouetted against the skylit rectangle of the window now, and a very fine silhouette she made, too. He forced his mind to concentrate on the exact meaning of her words.

E. J. continued: "I used the word 'immoral' because that was the impression I received during the conference."

"Impression?"

"That you consider the commercial exploitataion of Sterilin to be immoral."

Gorste frowned. "Not in so many words, E. J. Frankly I don't care what you do with the product once it has passed from the lab in a marketable form. But I thought some of the ideas put forward, particularly those to do with packaging, were rather objectionable . . . the compact idea, for instance. You can't market a medical product of this type in such a way."

"I can and I will," E. J. said crisply. "The moral climate of society is changing, Mr. Gorste, and changing quickly. And Sterilin itself will play an important part in stimulating the evolution of a more liberal morality."

"That's what I'm afraid of."

"Afraid of?" E. J. came closer, her eyes thoughtful. "You must not confuse morality with conscience."

Gorste smiled. "What's the difference? My conscience tells me what is moral and what is immoral."

E. J.'s eyebrows moved slightly, making her expression mildly quizzical. "Does it?" She crossed to the massive desk and stooped behind it, rummaging in an unseen cupboard. "Gin or whisky?" came her voice.

A succession of bottles began to appear on top of the desk. A siphon of soda water completed the array. Gorste watched in fascination at this unexpected conversion of the desk into a cocktail bar, and only when E. J. stood up and eyed him enquiringly did he remember her question.

"Gin," he murmured apologetically, wishing immediately that he had asked for whisky, for gin always seemed to him to be an effeminate drink, even though he preferred it.

"Tonic?"

"Please."

She poured two identical drinks, and Gorste went over to the desk to take his. They stood there for a while, in the pallid window light, standing quite close to each other and sipping the colorless biting fluid. He found himself holding the steady gaze of her dark eyes without embarrassment. It was as if they were beginning to understand each other.

"Let me explain one or two things," she said quietly. "This business of morality: It starts off as a condition imposed by society and it is based on one indisputable fact—that women are fertile. The object of social morality is to keep pregnancy within the husband-wife family relationship; in other words, to preserve the family unit, which is the basic component of any organized society."

Gorste nodded uncertainly.

"If you admit that, then it follows that any act which could result in extramarital pregnancy is antisocial and therefore immoral. Isn't that true of all relationships between men and women?"

"You mean . . . yes, I see what you mean. It could be true, I suppose. The only thing is that there can be a great deal of immorality which would not result in pregnancy because the people concerned have taken certain precautions."

"That is exactly my point, Mr. Gorste. The morality we are talking about was crystallized a long, long time ago when what you call certain precautions just weren't available, when all women were fertile, except on the naturally 'safe' days. The definition was clear cut in those times, and extra-marital pregnancy was a very real danger. Today, of course, there is no such danger, apart from the occasional, inevitable accident. Women can arrange their fertility to suit their own convenience, or, as is more often the case, men do the arranging for them."

Gorste finished his drink and E. J. promptly refilled his glass. "You're suggesting," he said, "that contraception is resulting in more and more extramarital relationships."

"And premarital. Do you doubt it?"

"Yes, I do," Gorste said firmly. "I don't think there has

been any slackening of morality during the past generation. If anything moral principles are higher."

"Is that the voice of your conscience speaking?"

"No, but I do believe in conscience; and there you have the real morality. People don't change internally, however much society might evolve."

"Let's sit down," E. J. suggested. She led the way to the settee, and Gorste followed her mechanically, nursing his glass and feeling just a little airy as the gin permeated his system. He sat beside her, reclining comfortably against the resilient back, his shoulder touching E. J.'s.

"Conscience," E. J. murmured, speaking confidentially, close to his ear, "is a simple matter of conditioning. As a scientist you should know that. It's a kind of distortion of the child mind induced by parental control, education, the instilling of a sense of what is right and wrong according to the standards of the day. The conscience of an aborigine would differ considerably from that of a big city man, and no doubt the conscience of an ancient Egyptian would vary widely from yours and mine. Even today moral conscience is largely a matter of geography. In the East a man may have four wives and feel perfectly pious about it; but in the West bigamy is a crime. So you see, Mr. Gorste, conscience is a variable quantity."

"All right," said Gorste pensively. "But what are you trying to prove?"

She placed a cool, smooth hand on his, and the shock of the contact vibrated momentarily through his body. "I'm not trying to prove anything. I'm trying to talk ordinary sense. And, of course, it all comes back to Sterilin."

"I thought it would."

"You think too much; that's your trouble, Mr. Gorste."

He looked at her, finding her face very close and her eyes mischievous. Her fingers tightened impulsively on his hand, but he resisted an impulse to return the token caress.

"Sterilin," she continued, "is going to accelerate the process of moral emancipation. After all, once you eliminate fertility, with one hundred per cent reliability, then the whole significance of sex is altered."

"Hedonism," Gorste remarked.

"No. Hedonism is essentially a defiance of conventional conduct—a kind of anarchy. Sterilin cannot produce Hedonism, but it may well disassociate sex from pregnancy, with ultimate benefit to the whole of mankind. There will inevitably be profound changes in morality . . . changes for the better."

"That is a point of view," Gorste conceded. "But contraceptives in one form or another have existed for longer than I have, and they haven't destroyed morality."

E. J. smiled enigmatically "Sterilin is different. It is a tablet, and it will last for six months; it has a long-term effect. The entire psychology of Sterilin administration is different, and the psychology of Sterilin users will be different, too."

"I think you're wrong, E. J"

"We shall see. Meanwhile, it is for you to go ahead and perfect Sterilin in tablet form. And it is for me to plan the commercial exploitation. I'm relying on you, Mr. Gorste."

Her voice, Gorste thought, was becoming husky, and the light from the window was failing as the heavy rain clouds moved sluggishly across the darkening sky. He placed his empty glass on the floor, and glanced at his watch.

"I suppose I ought to be getting back to the lab," he said uncertainly. "It has been a most interesting discussion, and I can see your point of view, though I don't necessarily agree with it."

He tried to stand up, but E. J. took his arms and pushed him back into the settee, very gently and too intimately. The blood beat in his head

"There's all the time in the world, Mr. Gorste," she whispered. "I haven't finished with you yet."

Gorste allowed himself to be seduced. He had known all along that it would finish this way, but his reluctance had been half-hearted from the beginning, and towards the end his own eagerness disgusted him. E. J. was exquisitely feminine, more so than he would have imagined, but she was also too smoothly professional, and her movements were those of a connoisseur, and he realized eventually that he had been exploited. The executive-employee relationship had not survived the first gin and tonic, and when it was all over he knew that he could no longer even remain an employee.

The first thing E. J. said—and it was an acrid question—was: "What price your moral conscience now, Mr. Gorste?"

Gorste sat beside her on the settee, biting his lip in the semidarkness. The thing was done and he felt sick and ashamed. The image of Anne hovered accusingly in the obscure depths of his mind. E. J. had proved her point: conscience was a conditioned veneer, and morality was a function of fertility—or sterility, whichever way you liked to look at it. He was sterile, and it might well have been the subconscious awareness of his advantageous incapacity that had weakened his resolve. After all, no harm had been done; there could be no physical repercussions in terms of pregnancy. But he knew that he was making excuses, and that he had been guilty of the supreme act of infidelity. Despite his moralizing and high-toned attitude, the big boss of Biochemix and future exploiter of Sterilin had made him eat his words here, in this very room, on this very settee.

Gorste's mind returned irrelevantly to the dead, dissected monkey in the laboratory. *Point of origin,* he thought. *Where is it all starting, this kind of licentious indulgence: in microtome sections of a simean ovary under a binocular microscope. And where will it finish, in the long run? In worldwide mass sterility artficially induced by Sterilin and its derivatives? In a rapidly falling birth rate? In an insidious de-*

cay of moral inhibitions, the destruction of conscience, an
irrevocable plunge into moral agnosticism . . . ?

"The word "amoral" checked his train of thought. It was a
concept he had overlooked in trying to define his own attitude to the problem of Sterilin and to what had so recently
taken place in this room. It was a loophole that he seized
upon momentarily with a distinct feeling of relief, for, of
course, amorality implied the nonrecognition of accepted moral standards and behavior. One had one's own standards, and
one acted in good faith in accordance with those standards,
acknowledging no higher authority. E. J.'s conduct, for instance, could hardly be defined as immoral since she was
aware of no conflict within herself, and there was no sense of
having sinned against some arbitrary bylaw of the soul imposed by conscience. She simply acted outside the pattern of
conventional morality, in a *bona fide* manner. She was amoral,
without a moral sense or code.

Gorste recognized that he was about to drive his own
mental turbulence into the comforting padded cell of amorality. For an instant he was almost the gay dog, uninhibited,
free to formulate his own rules of behavior, able to accept
whatever pleasures life might have to offer if he felt so in-
clined, with no sense of guilt or transgression. A moment
later he sensed that he was deceiving himself. Whatever
E. J.'s code of behavior might be, *his* was too rigidly defined. He was a married man, and he recognized the bonds
and barriers of marriage, and his conscience, conditioned or
not, was a very real thing. There might be such a thing as
amorality, but it wasn't for him. By his standards, the
amoral and the immoral were the same thing, and the relationship that now existed between himself and E. J. was
an evil thing within his own terms of reference.

E. J. left the settee and poured another drink for each of
them. Gorste accepted it silently.

"Nothing to say?" E. J. asked. "Not even thank you?"

Something cynical twisted the shape of his lips a little. "Thank you, for the drink," he murmured.

"Perhaps," she said thoughtfully, "you think of me as too sophisticated. It's not quite like that. I just look at life in a different way. I like to think that perhaps I can add something, however little, to the pleasure of living."

"For whom?"

"For all concerned. It takes two people to form a liaison of that kind. And, after all, Mr. Gorste, what is the motive? Pleasure, surely."

"Yes, but pleasure is not always a good motive . . ."

"It is neither good nor bad. It is the way one reacts to it that matters. In your case it is obviously a bad reaction, and you are worried; but it will pass. Next time the reaction will be less and the pleasure greater. That is how the human system adapts itself."

Gorste sipped his drink slowly. "There will be no next time, E. J. What I did was against my better judgment . . ."

She smiled in disbelief. "I don't remember hearing any protests. In fact you responded far more quickly and with a great deal more energy than many I could name. Why not forget about it? Push it out of your mind. Here and now at this moment it might never have happened."

Gorste stood up and placed the half empty glass on the desk. He stared out of the window into the rain. "I am resigning," he stated flatly. "I will let you have the usual formal notice of resignation in writing. One month's notice is required, I believe."

E. J. came over to him and stood behind him, putting her hands lightly on his shoulders.

"I won't accept your resignation, Mr. Gorste. And, in any case, you won't even submit it. By tomorrow you'll feel quite differently . . ."

"It has nothing to do with you, or what happened in here, E. J. It's well, I no longer have faith in my work. I can no longer believe that what I am doing is right, or even desirable. I'm afraid I can't stop Sterilin at this stage; the work is too advanced. Slade can pick up where I leave off."

He turned round to face her, his eyes solemn.

"I just want to wash my hands of the whole damned business."

E. J. eyed him shrewdly. In the cold, flat light from the window she looked older now, and there were fine lines around her mouth and under her eyes.

"All right," she said. "Resign if you wish. After all, you can always withdraw your resignation within the next four weeks."

"I'm afraid you don't really understand me, E. J.," said Gorste.

E. J. nodded slowly. "I think I do. The real trouble, Mr. Gorste, is that you don't understand yourself."

IX

ANNE had to be told, of course. Now that he had assumed the pose of righteousness (and it *was* a pose, he realized, but an essential pose to provide a kind of spiritual stability, and fill some indefinable vacuum in his emotional make-up), he had to be consistent in himself and follow it through. It would hurt Anne considerably, and so little did he know her that he found himself unable to predict her reaction. Would she become cold and silent and malevolent, or would she be consumed in vindictive fury? Or, more happily, would she remain calm and talk about the situation reasonably and understandingly as he himself would try to do.

Surprisingly, when he arrived home, the television set had not been switched on. Anne was reading the evening paper without much interest, and the moment he came into the room she put it down and came over to him and kissed him.

It was almost as if she had sensed what had happened and was anxious to dismiss his fears.

Gorste, obsessed by the events of the day, came to the point immediately. He said: "I've resigned my job, darling."

She looked at him blankly for a moment, as if something she had been about to say had suddenly been pushed out of her mind.

"I had to resign," he went on. "I came to the conclusion that it would be unethical to continue on the research program. It's a long-term question of morality."

"Morality," she echoed, puzzled. "Phil, I don't think you ought to resign. It's a good, secure job and you're well paid. You can't resign—not just yet."

"What exactly do you mean: 'not just yet'?"

She hesitated, then smiled coyly. "Well, darling, I've got a secret for you. I wasn't sure until today." A brief pause while she kissed him lightly on the lips. "We're going to have a baby."

Gorste said nothing, just stood rigidly holding her.

"So you see why you can't resign, Phil. You're going to need that job, and we're going to need all the money we can get. We have to move out of the flat, perhaps buy a house. We can't take any chances with our baby's future, can we?"

As Gorste made no response, she moved away from him and regarded him anxiously. "What's the mateer, darling?" she asked. "Aren't you pleased?"

He seemed to come alive, as if someone had pressed a switch. "Of course," he murmured vaguely, then went over to an armchair and sat down. Anne followed, sitting on the floor, curling herself up against his knees.

"You're worried about something, Phil. Please tell me."

He was looking at her strangely, as if he had never seen her before. His voice when he spoke was quiet and toneless.

"You're quite sure about the baby?"

"Yes. I saw the doctor today. Another six months, he said."

"Anne, I've left you on your own a great deal during the past few months. There have been evenings when I've had to work late . . ."

"It's all right, darling. I've never complained, have I?"

"What I mean is, well, I've always trusted you, Anne . . ."

She looked up at him with wide, questioning eyes. "Philip, what on earth . . . ?"

He chose his words carefully. "You see, it's this way. I can't possibly be the father of your child. I'm sterile."

Her face, her expression, became transfixed. Slowly she stood up, holding on to the mantelpiece for support.

"Philip, you're talking nonsense. Of course you're the father. You don't imagine . . . ?"

"Nor did your first husband. Drewin never imagined that you were being unfaithful."

Her face, paler now, was taut and suddenly older. The knuckles of the hand that held the mantelpiece gleamed white through the skin.

She said slowly: "For God's sake, Philip, things were different then: I hated Drewin and I loved you. There has never been anyone else."

"I'm sterile, and it was Drewin who made me that way," Gorste stated factually. "He did it with radioactive isotopes; so you can't be having my child. It's just not possible."

"You're terribly mistaken, Philip," she said, more calmly. "I don't believe you're sterile. I know about what Drewin did. He told me just before I killed him; that was why I killed him. He said he knew about us and that I was wasting my time because he'd fixed things so that you'd never be a man again . . ."

"You *killed* him . . ." Gorste echoed in cold consternation.

Anne came nervously towards him and knelt down by his chair. He remained remote and frigid. She said: "I didn't mean to tell you ever. It—it slipped out. But it's true, Phil.

I killed him for what he had done to you. I killed him so that we could be together . . ."

"It was suicide. He gassed himself."

"He'd been drinking heavily one night. He wanted coffee. I put four sleeping tablets in it. When he was unconscious I dragged him into the kitchen, and, well, . . . I'm not sorry, darling; I've never regretted it."

Gorste stood up, leaving her kneeling by the chair, and paced heavily across the room. "You murdered your husband," he said hollowly. "You were unfaithful to him and then you murdered him."

Anger began to flush into Anne's face. She stood up slowly, staring intently at Gorste who, still pacing the floor, took care not to look at her.

"You talk," she said, "as if you never had anything to do with it. If I was unfaithful it was because of you. If I hadn't killed Drewin we wouldn't have been married now."

"What appalls me is that it's happening all over again," said Gorste in a thin strained voice. "You've been playing around with some other man behind my back, and you're having his child. You thought you could pass it off as mine, but it won't work. How long will it be before you decide to murder me, too? How long?"

"You fiend!"

"Coming from you that's funny. I just can't believe it; that you could actually kill a man in cold blood. There wasn't even a fight or an argument. You doped his coffee, then pushed his head in the gas oven. That's about as cold-blooded as you can get."

"So . . . what are you going to do about it?"

Gorste looked at her for the first time in minutes. His face was a mask; there was hate in his eyes. "We're through, Anne. I don't want an unfaithful wife, and I won't protect a murderess. Get out and go to your lover. Get out! That's all."

"You're a stupid fool, Philip," she said angrily. "There isn't any lover, and what I did was for you. Can't you get that into your thick skull?"

"You're a liar," he said firmly.

She lost control of herself at that point, and flung herself at him, beating at his face with clenched fists, and biting his wrists as he tried to restrain her. And the tears came abruptly, and crying and moaning she tried to hurt the man who she felt had hurt her. Gorste became angry and struck at her. She fell, caught her head against the edge of the coffee table, and lay still.

When he had confirmed that she was dead, Gorste's first reaction was to telephone for the police. He dialed the first three digits without feeling, his mind drained of all thought or emotion. Then he hesitated and replaced the phone.

It was an accident, of course. He hadn't deliberately tried to kill her or hurt her in any way. She had slipped—the rest had been inevitable.

What would the average man have done? It was an accident and he would not have wasted time in confirming death. He would have called a doctor; then the doctor could call the police if he thought it necessary.

He picked up the phone again and dialed a number. The doctor's voice came over the line.

"This is Philip Gorste, I—"

"Ah, Mr. Gorste," interrupted the doctor cheerfully, "I've been meaning to ring you. The lab report came in today. You know, about your sterility test. . . . You were wrong, completely wrong!"

"Meaning?" said Gorste, hardly able to concentrate on the other's words.

"Meaning you're not sterile and never were sterile. No reason why you shouldn't have a family of twenty if you wish. Unless, perhaps, your wife . . ."

"Yes, my wife," Gorste echoed bitterly.

"Perhaps I ought to examine her, just to make sure. Not

that she's sterile, but sometimes there can be a slight physical impediment which can be corrected."

"She's sterile enough, and there's nothing you or anyone else can do about it. You'd better come over and examine her right now."

The doctor hesitated an instant, as if he had detected some strange and convincing inflexion in Gorste's voice. Then he said: "I'll be there without delay, Mr. Gorste. Give me five minutes."

Gorste hung up dejectedly, then lifted the phone again and dialed the police.

PART THREE

THE GIRL

X

THE big flame-colored letters of the neon sign spelled Sterilin. Each letter was a convoluted glass tube fifty feet tall, and the word was clamped high on the wall of the Wasserman building, glaring its message into the night like a danger beacon. It dominated Piccadilly Circus, swamping all the other neon lights in its vicinity. You could see it from across the river, and on a clear night the letters of the word could be made out from the top of the Microwave Tower in Highgate, nearly six miles away.

But tonight visibility was not good. The sign peered harshly through a semi-opaque curtain of persistent drizzle, frustrated and confined, but seeking compensation in the wet surface of the road where the reflection, broken and shimmering

in the rain film, echoed glowing fragments of the word—
Sterilin.

Piccadilly Circus was almost deserted. The rain had sent
the evening pleasure seekers scuttling into movies and thea-
ters and restaurants. There was not much traffic. Drivers
whose destination lay beyond the West End preferred the
metallic air-conditioned luxury of the Metrocircle Tunnel with
its four-lane, plastic-surfaced road, or the wide ambitious
highway of the elevated Central Bypass, poised like an in-
finite bridge across the tops of the taller buildings.

The statue of Eros was floodlit, as it had been for the
past half century. The arrow no longer pointed towards
Shaftesbury Avenue; instead it was aimed accurately at the
gigantic Sterilin sign. The change in orientation had been surreptitiously introduced some four or five years ago, and few
people realized that Sir Bernard Wasserman was behind it
Sir Bernard had, in fact, pulled a few influential wires, and
the statue had been turned on its pedestal one night to face
and complement the message of the neon sign. Eros and
Sterilin: symbols of the early years of the twenty-first century, if you stopped to think about it, but not many people
bothered to think at all. They were too busy being happy.

It was part of Brad Somer's job to do a great deal of thinking, however. But not tonight. Wasserman wasn't on his
mind, nor was he consciously aware of the giant word glaring incandescently at him through the rain. It was simply one
of the things you took for granted, a part of the Piccadilly
decor, as familiar and unremarkable as the Guinness clock in
years gone by; and not only in Piccadilly, for Sterilin, in
scarlet neon, could be seen in most main roads and streets
in most cities and towns in the country or in the world.

He was waiting for a girl. Six or seven other men were
waiting for girls, too. It was a popular occupation in the age
of atomics and automation and applied happiness. They were
all standing on the island at the center of Piccadilly Circus,

under the luminous shadow of Eros, becoming progressively
wetter as each minute passed by. Occasionally they eyed
each other covertly, and each looked cold and damp and
treasonably miserable, out of key in this ecstatic world of
2021. But it was only a temporary modulation of mood
brought about by the weather. In due course, and one by one,
came the girls, and the transient gloom of the patient males
dispersed like fine frost in morning sunshine.

Somer's girl was late, and soon he was alone on the island.
It continued to rain and he continued to wait. The raindrops
bounced and pattered on the shining wet road, creating
ephemeral craters that came and went like snapshots. Cars
sighed and they sped wearily past, throwing a gentle spray
into the air from hooded wheels.

He looked idly around A flashing green sign in the direction of Regent Street announced: *Kill Bad Breath! Chew
Choosy, the Chic Chicle*. Adjacent to it the outline of a nude
woman in amber glowed intermittently in the darkness, al-
ternating with a vivid blue phrase that said: *Eat Here and
View*. And beyond that, enigmatically traced in white and
crimson: *You Want It! We Have It!* And more and more
neon signs advertising gasoline, movies, haircream, lingerie,
cars, nylons, perfumes, gyrojet services, beers, wines, spirits,
cigarettes, and all the other desirable amenities of civilization. And, remotely visible over the dark shoulder of a semi-
skyscraper, a luminous pointing hand with the bold legend:
God Needs You Need God. But nobody ever bothered to
look at the neons . . . unless he happened to be waiting for
a girl.

There was no hurry, Somer told himself. He could wait until midnight if necessary. In any case there was an even
chance that she wouldn't turn up on the basis of a casual
invitation by telephone. If it came to the point he might not
even recognize her, for the description she had given of
herself was vague; on the other hand he was wearing the

agreed symbol of identity: two carnations, crimson and white, side by side, in his buttonhole.

The rain did not bother him overmuch. The transparent waterproof cape he was wearing kept him dry and fairly warm; only his feet felt chilled and uncomfortable. He abandoned the neons and watched the passing cars—squat streamlined shapes progressing with effortless and sinister motion on almost invisible wheels. The atomic drives of the newer and more expensive models were virtually noiseless. And inside were the inevitable women, frilly and glistening like Christmas fairy dolls, with the men crouched hollow-eyed and intent over the driving wheel. Gay women and somber men, using the supernal power of the atom to carry them as rapidly as possible to a centrally heated room and a soft resilient bed.

Applied happiness, Somer thought cynically. *If I weren't what I am, I'd be the same as the rest of the men. I'd want a car with atomic drive, and a luxury flat equipped with vidarphone, and a big bank balance, and shares in the Sterilin combine, and a regular lower-level female, sucking cinnamon and smelling faintly of gin, and two or three higher-level females for prestige. I'd be in the stallion class, with an office high up in the Mall, overlooking the big statue of E. J. Wasserman herself, the founder of Sterilin, and I'd be signing papers and lifting a telephone and making eyes at a raven-haired secretary (with her Sterilin card stamped up-to-date); and life would seem very secure and stable, with only increasing prosperity and happiness in store.*

On the surface, of course; only on the surface But the others could not even begin to suspect the truth . . .

Rona came presently. She had crossed the road by the subway so that she materialized unexpectedly behind Somer First thing he knew, there was a husky feminine voice behind him that said: "Red and white add up to Brad. Right?"

He turned round and looked her over. She was wearing a plastic cape with a hood, and it was translucent enough to show the outline of her short black dress and the long white curve of her legs. Her hair matched the flame color of the Sterilin sign. Her lips were carmine and moist from the rain, and her green eyes seemed to possess an internal fire of their own. She was nice to look at, and probably nicer still to kiss.

"You must be Rona," he said.

She nodded. "Let's get out of this rain."

"The Waldorf?"

"Anywhere."

He took her arm and conducted her towards a taxi stand. "No car?"

'In America. I may have it sent over if I decide to stay."

"You ought to, Brad. Otherwise you don't rate."

They took a cab to the Waldorf and settled down in the cocktail bar After the rain the ornate and elegantly fashioned room was a virtual paradise.

"What'll it be, Rona?"

"Whisky."

"With?"

"Dry."

Somer snapped his fingers at the bartender. "Scotch and dry twice."

"So you know Lecia?" Rona said.

"Yes. For many years. She suggested I should contact you. I hope I didn't do the wrong thing."

"Not at all, Brad. But I'm curious. Is there an angle, or are you just dating me?"

"Both. I'd be a heel not to date a girl like you."

"Business before pleasure. What's the angle?"

He paid for the drinks and they both sipped. "All in good time, Rona. You're a pretty girl . . . more than pretty."

"You're an American. You ought to know."

"Right. I've traveled around a great deal, most everywhere. Being an American doesn't make me a connoisseur of women, but I've seen plenty of them and had more than I'd like to count without an electronic calculater. You're in the very top bracket, honey."

"Corny, Brad. It sounds like a typical opening gambit."

"Would you like it in writing?"

"No. I'd like it in bed."

Somer smiled. "Don't rush me. I was born in Idaho and I take things slowly."

"What's your line of business, Brad," Rona asked, finishing her drink.

He had the glasses refilled before answering. "I'm a journalist."

"Radio or TV?"

"Newspaper."

Her lip curled imperceptibly. "Does anyone read newspapers these days?"

"Surprisingly, yes. More than a million people in America; more than a quarter of a million in Britain."

"Of course, Lecia was a journalist for a time, before she joined the Ministry of the Written Word. She didn't like it much—being a journalist, I mean."

"Who does? It's a frame of mind. Hard work, too. Nowadays you have to dig deep to get at facts and figures. Co-operation is hard to come by."

Rona examined her long, oval fingernails with a remotely critical air. "Is that why Lecia told you to contact me?"

"That was the general idea."

"Any friend of Lecia is a friend of mine—up to a point. You have to remember I'm a government official, Brad."

"See what I mean about co-operation?"

"No, I'm not being awkward. I'd like to know more about you, about your assignment, about the kind of information you're after."

"With pleasure, honey, but not here. There are too many people around." He glanced at his watch. "I've a nice comfortable hotel room just four stories above our heads. How about it?"

She smiled, and there was a hint of cynicism in the curve of her lips. "Wonderful, Brad. But I've got a better idea. Let's go to my flat. You'll like it. We can pick up a bottle of something on the way."

"You talked me into it," he said.

It was not a big flat, but it was modern and pleasing to the eye. The air in the living room was maintained exactly at a temperature of 72 degrees Fahrenheit summer and winter—not too cool to be bracing and not too warm to be relaxing. One entire wall was a window of chrome glass, polarized so that it was opaque from outside and transparent from within. The ceiling was an opalescent rectangle bounded by walls, and it came alight all over when the wall switch was depressed. The hue and brilliance could be controlled independently by milled knobs recessed in the switch panel. The walls were beige in a matt cellulose finish. The furniture was simple, but adequate; two dark green chairs of molded flexible plastic, and a glass table on spindly legs of drawn steel. There was also a small folding divan of airfoam latex. Surprisingly there were no immediately discernible indications of feminine occupation: no flowers or drapes or trimmings.

Rona unlocked the door and led the way in, switching on the luminous ceiling to give a warm, subdued rose-colored glow which, as she had learned from experience, made women look flushed and lovelier and men appear tanned and impassioned.

She removed her cape and preened herself a little in front of Somer. She had plenty to preen about by contemporary standards, he thought. Her dress was made from one of the latest spun synthetic polyestomer compounds. It was black and gossamer, not much larger than a swimsuit, with a short frilled skirt that stopped a few inches above her knees. Her legs were encased in sheer stockings, transparent to the point of invisibility, apart from the smooth eggshell glaze they imparted to her skin. At the top of each stocking, partly concealed by the black skirt, was a group of words in tiny green lettering. They were too far away to decipher.

Her shoes were black to match her dress, and cut away like string sandals. Her toenails were silver, as were her fingernails. They could have been chromium plated.

Presently Somer got around to looking at her face. It was a nice face: oval, regular, with warm generous lips. Her hair, tawny and a little awry after its release from the restricting hood, was long and thick, with a deep natural wave. Even in the diffused light from the ceiling it had an incredible sheen.

"Make yourself at home," said Rona.

Somer removed his cape and unloaded a bottle of whisky from his pocket. Rona put the capes in an adjacent room, then returned to deposit herself neatly in the divan. She patted the vacant space beside her.

"Sit down, Brad."

He sat down and they kissed formally. It was like shaking hands.

"Drink?"

She nodded.

Somer fixed two whiskies and returned to the divan. They touched glasses.

"To all beautiful girls with auburn hair," he said.

She smiled. "To all mysterious men with strange, dark eyes."

They drank a little and embraced lightly.

"In the ordinary way," she said, "I wouldn't have to stop and think about a thing. People don't have to think much

these days. Life goes according to formula. You're here and
I'm here and we've both been trained."

"What's so different this time?" he asked.

"The fact that you've got a motive. What exactly is it you
want, Brad?"

"You mean apart from you?"

She nodded.

"Well, Rona honey, it's a long story. As a journalist I'm
always looking for a story, but you know how things are
today. Radio and television monopolize the news and information services, and newspapers are at a disadvantage. Circu-
lations have fallen to critical levels. A couple of generations
ago there used to be more than fifty million newspaper
readers in America. Now there are only one million. In
order to survive we have to be different. We have to be independent. We think in terms of scoops and exposures and
investigations. We're yellower than the yellowest press of
the last century."

"What paper do you work for, Brad?"

"The *United States Sentinel*. One of the only three national
scale newspapers still in existence over there. And, incidentally, it may surprise you to know that the *Sentinel* owns
Britain's biggest circulation daily—the *National Mirror*."

"I don't seem to care awfully."

"Well, this is just background stuff. The point is that newspapers are few and far between, and they only survive because they stick their necks out."

"I never knew newspapers had necks."

"Maybe not. But journalists have."

"So what are you trying to prove?"

"I'm darned if I know, honey. I'm gathering facts, and I'm
hoping the facts will add up to a story. If they do, it's going
to be the most sensational story of all time."

"Such as . . . ?"

Somer grinned wrily. "Like another drink?"

"Why not?"

He took the empty glasses and refilled them. Rona was growing lethargic, reclining langorously, her lips slightly parted, her eyes dreamy but glistening—hypnotically alert.

"During the past two or three years there has been a sudden increase in opposition to the independent newspapers," Somer continued. "You must remember that all the radio and television information services are controlled by the government. The only news medium that is free of censorship is the press, what is left of it. Even the British *National Mirror* has become a government organ; it survives on official handouts. The reporters are gagged."

"So what has it to do with me?"

"I'm coming to that in my own way. You see, Rona, censorship means there's something to hide. And my assignment is to find out exactly what is being hidden?"

"But why come to England?"

"Because this is where censorship and governmental blackout is at its worst. This is where Sterilin first started. And this is where the answer is to be found."

Rona sighed. "Brad, you seem to have a chip on your shoulder, and I'm darned if I can understand what it's all about, or what I have to do with it. Couldn't we talk business later? I'm being frustrated. I never knew a man to frustrate me so much."

Somer sipped his drink then put the glass down "I'm sorry, honey," he said. "I guess I'm putting the cart before the horse."

He pulled her towards him quite suddenly and kissed her with professional know-how. She molded herself to the shape of him.

"That's better," she murmured.

"But I have to talk to you later."

"Why do you *have* to?"

"It's vitally important, Rona. Not only for us, but for the entire human race."

Her lips touched his gently for a moment. "You talk too much, Brad."

He whispered: "We'll take it up later." Then he embraced her tightly and automatically practiced phase one of the prescribed procedure of the International College of Erotic Culture. Rona seemed to melt in his arms. Presently he got around to reading the green lettering at the top of her stockings.

It said: *If you can read this you're too close.*

XI

"WAS Lecia nicer than me?" Rona asked felinely.

He considered. "She was different."

"All women are different. Didn't you know, darling?"

"Some are more different than others."

She pouted. "What the hell do you mean by that?"

He put a languid arm around her. "I mean that you're more different than most."

"In what way?"

"I can't find the right word. Something fundamental. So many women these days take lovemaking as a matter of routine. Somehow you don't, Rona. You make it personal . . . intimate."

"That's the way it should be, Brad. You're not so bad yourself." She paused, eyeing him speculatively.

"You going to stay the night?" she asked.

"Is that what you want?"

She nodded slowly.

"Well, Rona, it depends on you. I came here for a reason. If you're co-operative the way I want, then I'll stay."

For a few moments she eyed him coldly and laconically.

"Why is it men are so damned independent these days, as though they were some kind of master race?"

Brad smiled. "Perhaps it has to do with supply and demand. Men are getting scarcer every day. You ought to know."

"Why ought I?"

"Because you work in the Department of Statistics. You see all the official governmental documents You're five years ahead of the press."

"Is that why Lecia told you to contact me?"

"That's why. Sorry?"

"Not particularly. But I can't help you, Brad. I'm a government official. I'm under an oath of secrecy."

He snapped his fingers "It doesn't mean a thing. It depends where your loyalties lie: whether you want to be a robot in the service of another robot, or whether you want to serve a living humanity."

She regarded him with a puzzled air, frowning. "I don't see what you're getting at, Brad You're talking politics."

"This is more than politics, Rona It's life and death, and you know it."

"You'd better explain," she said.

He explained: "It began in the second half of the twentieth century, when a chemical combine known as Biochemix Incorporated introduced a new contraceptive product called Sterilin on the market. Supported by shrewd advertising and attractive, glamorous packaging (the tablets were contained in a handbag-size gilt compact), Sterilin rapidly became the leading product of its kind, with sales rocketing to fabulous figures. Each tablet of Sterilin was capable of inducing absolute sterility in a woman for not less than six months The result was a new kind of emancipation for the female sex. Pregnancy was virtually abolished overnight. Women, slowly, cautiously at first, but later with gathering momentum, began to exploit their new found freedom from the centuries old fear of accidental conception.

"Ten years after the first Sterilin advertisement appeared in a leading woman's magazine, an obscure government statistician produced a significant document. In Great Britain, America and Europe, and in all countries where Sterilin had been intensively marketed, according to the report, birth rates had fallen alarmingly. Worse still, there had been a snowballing deterioration in the moral standards of civilized society. Marriage was rapidly losing all meaning. Promiscuity was becoming the accepted pattern of behavior. Protected by Sterilin, women no longer saw any point in resisting the more pleasurable temptations of life, and men, who needed little encouragement anyway, stormed the collapsing barriers of feminine virtue with aggressive determination and were delighted to find their invasion more than welcome.

"The British government, disconcerted by the statistician's report, decided to go into action, and forthwith appointed a Royal Commission to investigate the overall result on society of the introduction of Sterilin, with particular reference to the problem of the falling birth rate. Unfortunately all of the members of the Commission were themselves, directly or indirectly, grateful users of Sterilin, and they never reached a finding.

"The United States of America adopted a more forthright approach: without bothering to investigate, Congress immediately slapped a prohibitive tax on Sterilin tablets. Sales dropped overnight, then slowly began to pick up. Revenue derived from the tax grew and grew to immense proportions, and when Sterilin sales eventually returned to their original level, the United States government found that they had unwittingly acquired a new and lucrative source of internal revenue even exceeding that yielded by tobacco and alcoholic drinks combined.

"The British government, followed by various European

governments, promptly imitated America's example, anxious too, to combine a superficial disapproval of Sterilin with a fabulous increase in tax revenue. The Soviet Union, never willing to copy the decadent methods of the West, banned Sterilin by government edict, but deliberately omitted to implement the ban, then compensated by imposing extortionate fines of all convicted of purchasing Sterilin tablets in the black market. The end result in terms of revenue was much the same as if they had imposed a tax.

"Eastern races, for whom overpopulation had always been a problem, saw in Sterilin a medium by which population could be controlled and, in consequence, living standards raised. In China, Japan, Indian and Pakistan Sterilin therapy was actually encouraged by the government, who even went so far as to subsidize the drug so as to bring it within the price range of the multitude. For the truly penniless Sterilin centers were set up where prophylactic doses could be obtained free of charge.

"The truth was that the world was confused in its reaction to Sterilin. The people welcomed it; some governments were sternly disapproving; the Church was horrified, and many nations gave it authoritative backing. And as the years went by the birth rate continued to fall, and morality crumbled away In the course of a decade there was hardly a human female anywhere in the world whose ovaries had not been artificially put out of action.

"Meanwhile, as the problem of the falling birth rate became more and more serious, governments took various ineffective measures to control the use of the drug. France, for instance, nationalized the local Sterilin plant, and then, being French, not only failed to close down the factory, but proceeded to build new factories. This was because no government in France was ever able to survive long enough to oppose the desire of the people. In any case, having taken over the exploitation of Sterilin in France, the government found the venture too profitable to consider seriously restricting its commercial distribution.

"In the end the growing crisis reached United Nations level, and so began months of fruitless discussion around shiny conference tables while political leaders of the world argued on a subject they knew very little about: the ethics of contraception and what to do about it.

"The answer came from Russia, who, presumably, had viewed the situation through dialectical spectacles. The Soviet delegate pointed out that it would be impracticable to ban the use of Sterilin unless the new uninhibited behavior pattern of male-female relationships could be banned also. Promiscuity, indeed, a pervading amorality of society, had come to stay, and if Sterilin were banned, then people would simply resort to other forms of birth control, including abortion. There would be a surge of illegal operations performed, no doubt, by quack doctors, but amorality would continue. Habits of thought and conduct, once established, are difficult to eradicate even on an individual basis; on a national or planetary basis—impossible.

"On the other hand, the delegate went on, the declining birth rate was a threat to the future of human life which had to be dealt with here and now. It was an emergency, and it called for prompt action. Governments could not dictate the morals of their peoples, but they could define the duties and responsibilities of their subjects. It was the prime duty of every woman, the delegate declared, to bear children in order to maintain the national birth rate at a stable level.

"He then made the following proposals: Laws must be created and enforced to compel every woman of mature age to spend a period in what might be termed a fertility center, where she would be impregnated and made to bear a child; the number of children each woman would be required to bear during adult life would depend on existing birth rate statistics: it might be three or four.

"Since the family as a unit had largely disintegrated and sexual irresponsibility was the accepted order of things, governments might be required to accept responsibility for the rearing and educating of all children born at the official fertility centers. This would necessitate the establishment of State nurseries and schools.

"The entire project must be ruthlessly organized and applied. There must be severe fines, even imprisonment, for women failing to co-operate. The children born must be shepherded by the State, for the family influence was no longer effective or desirable. Only in this way could the slump in the birth rate be checked, and stability injected into the matter of human procreation.

"The Soviet delegate's proposal had a mixed reception, mainly because the other delegates at the conference felt vaguely resentful that they hadn't thought of it first. Protests were made; delegates spoke heatedly of totalitarian dictatorship, of breeding kennels, of a mechanistic approach to the sacred act of human propagation, of profane materialism, and of sheer defilement of the human spirit; but after the rhetoric and argument had blown itself out, one fact remained starkly evident; that there was no other practicable solution to the problem.

"And so Sterilin remained, and the nations of the world set about regimenting the female sex under the compulsion of law, and built fertility centers and State nurseries and State schools, and laid the foundations for a new kind of human reproduction—childbirth by decree and conscription!"

"But I know all this," Rona complained, pouting sulkily. "I spent nearly the whole of last year in a fertility center. I had twins, but one died soon after birth." She frowned reminiscently. "It was horrible. Why can't we stay sterile all the time and have fun?"

"I've just told you, darling," Brad said patiently. "If everyone stayed sterile the human race would come to a sudden full stop."

"Why can't they sterilize the men?"

"Possibly they could. There's no point. Sterilin is harmless and perfectly efficient. In any case, women would still have to bear children in order that the race might survive."

"I think it's unfair, Brad. What does it matter, anyway? You and me, we shan't worry if the race comes to an end after we're dead."

"True, my dear. But politicians tend to take a long-term view."

There was an interval of silence while he poured fresh drinks. The hand holding the bottle shook slightly, splashing whisky on the table. He cursed silently. Hardened drinker though he was, he realized that the stuff was affecting his judgment. And Rona was growing restive, as if willing to exchange conversation for romantic ardor for a while. He resigned himself to the inevitable.

Half an hour later he said: "Getting back to more sordid matters, darling, this child of yours, was it a girl?"

"Yes."

"I thought so."

"Why do you say that?"

"I've been checking up, in my own way, over a long time, Rona. It may be a State secret, but I know."

"Know what?"

"That ninety-eight out of every hundred births are female, and that if the trend continues we shall soon reach the stage where all births are female. Boys just aren't being born any more."

"You're not supposed to know that," she said carefully.

"Don't tell *me*. I'm a journalist. Ever since the Russian plan for fertility centers was adopted more than twenty years ago, censorship has clamped down on vital information. The government has gradually taken control of the news and information services. The common people of the world are living in a kind of dream, with news made to measure in order to sustain the dream. You ought to know, Rona."

She eyed him solemnly. "Yes, I know, Brad."

"It started, I guess, from necessity. State fertility centers, nurseries, and so on; the kind of thing that might arouse a violent public reaction. Propaganda of the right kind was essential, and the newspapers and other news services were made to toe the line. That was the thin end of the wedge. Even so everything might have been okay, but it started happening . . ."

"It . . . ?"

"The sex compensation process."

"You *have* been checking up."

"That's why I've come to you, Rona. I'm on to a big story, perhaps the biggest of all time. But I need facts. My editor will print this story once it's authenticated. It may be the last edition of the paper ever, but at least we shall get the truth to nearly a quarter of a million readers, and they will talk, and it may be that the news will spread round the world . . ."

"Is that what you want?"

Brad grinned sardonically. "I'm the old-fashioned kind of journalist. I believe in telling the people the truth—the real truth—good or bad, whether the government likes it or not. I'm opposed to censorship, official handouts, secrecy in any form, and I defy embargoes on information that should be public domain."

She regarded him steadily. "That is treasonable talk, Brad."

"Treason? Sure; today that's the way it is. You know what, honey? We're living in a police state, the kind they used to have in the mid-twentieth century. Only it's more subtle. It's operated in terms of fertility centers and State nurseries and the Ministry of the Written Word and the Ministry of Statistics. But there isn't any noticeable relationship between the statistics and the written word. Am I right?"

"I wouldn't know, Brad. And I could use another drink.

He poured more whisky, a blockbusting dose for Rona and a homeopathic sample for himself. Funny about that girl—how she could drink and drink without reacting. Unless, and for an instant suspicion trembled in his brain, she had received an anti-alcoholic injection earlier in the day (a privilege reserved for government officials on important business, where balance of mind and judgment was imperative). He was afraid that the suspicion might have showed briefly in his eyes, but her expression betrayed nothing. Nevertheless an indefinable sense of caution darkened his mind.

She said: "All right, Brad, what information do you want from me?"

"The answers to four key questions, Rona. First: actual birth statistics showing the increase in female births over male. Second: statistics showing the decrease in numbers of youthful men, that is men under thirty, during the past twenty years. Third: information about recent experiments in artificial insemination and experiments in artificial parthenogenesis. Fourth: electronic brains."

Rona laughed abruptly. "Hell, Brad, what an imagination you have. Read any good science-fiction lately?"

"You know what I'm talking about, honey."

"Even if I did, I couldn't talk about it. You know that."

Brad took her in his arms, resisting an impulse to kiss her. "That's the routine line of talk, honey. Like you'd give to any nosey journalist. But I'm a more personal contact. We've got Lecia in common. You can talk to me."

"It would be more than my job is worth."

"Nobody need know. A reputable newspaper never divulges the source of its information."

"It would take time, Brad. Anyway, where did you dig up

this stuff from, about insemination and parthenogenesis, and electronic brains?"

"Knowing a few people in the right places."

"Like me?"

"Could be."

She eyed him shrewdly. "What people, for instance?"

"Why should you care, Rona?"

"I like to know I'm in good company before I sell my soul."

He shrugged, a little puzzled at some enigmatic quality in her attitude. "You're in exceptional company, honey. At least two names that are world famous, people who are opposed to the State policy of secrecy and this present-day obsession with security. They co-operated."

"So you've got your story anyway."

"I've got a general picture of what's happening behind the scenes, but I need factual confirmation. Official government figures to prove my point."

She lay back on the divan, regarding him from low angle with hazy eyes. "What point?"

He sighed patiently. "I've been telling you most of the evening, Rona."

"You told me the background, but not the big scoop you're working on. Before I make any promises I'd like to be sure that you're on the right track. It would be rather awkward if I gave you secret information you hadn't asked for; I mean, naturally, that I should want to keep the risk to a minimum."

"Reasonable," he murmured thoughtfully.

"In any case, Brad, until you give me a clear idea of what your story is about I can't be sure what information to get for you. The Department of Statistics contains four thousand filing cabinets, nearly a million microfilms, and twelve electronic memory banks. I've got to know precisely what data you require."

He glanced briefly at the wall clock: the time was eleven

thirty. Soon, he thought, we shall be sleeping together, and tomorrow she will do as I wish. She is suspicious, but not too much so, and she will co-operate in the end. For the moment I must do as she asks.

He lay down beside her and ran his fingers lightly over her. She trembled involuntarily. "Don't go to sleep," he murmured. "I'll tell you my story."

"Even when the first fertility centers were being constructed," he said quietly, "that section of the civil service that concerns itself with births, deaths and marriages became aware of a certain worrying trend in birth figures, something quite apart from the birth rate itself, which had fallen to a fantastically low level. It became disconcertingly apparent that of the babies being born, more and more were female. Whereas in pre-Sterilin days the ratio of male to female births was approximately fifty-fifty, the balance was now changing. At the time when the thing was discovered and confirmed beyond all dispute there were eight girls born to every boy.

"The information was censored, the first large-scale example of the suppression of vital information. Scientists were appointed to investigate the phenomenon, and they, in turn, finding themselves involved in complex social mathematics, enlisted the aid of giant electronic computors. And so the electronic brain began to enter the scene as an instrument of government policy.

"The new system of compulsory fertility worked, though not without some initial public protest. Women, under threat of large fines and imprisonment, reported to the centers, and were generally delighted to find that far from resembling maternity hospitals they were vast and luxurious rest centers set in spacious, secluded grounds in the rural areas of the country. Every facility for amusement and entertainment was provided for, and life, during the period of pregnancy, was idle and pleasurable.

"For the purposes of impregnation they were, during the first few years, permitted to select their own male partner; but later the government, in consultation with the electronic brains, decided to apply eugenic methods to human breeding. Male partners were selected according to scientific genetic principles, and the act of mating became a precision function with little or no emotional content. Once fertilization of the ovum had been achieved, complete promiscuity was, of course, then permissible.

"During this phase in the development of the fertility centers, certain quarters in the buildings were assigned to men, who had been eugenically selected for what might be called stud purposes. Men still lived at the fertility centers, but the trend in recent years has been towards artificial insemination, partly because of the greater certainty of precise eugenic breeding, and partly for another more sinister reason. Meanwhile the eugenically approved men, having made their contribution to the impersonal insemination machinery, were retained as a form of amusement for the women during their pregnancy.

"The move towards artificial insemination had resulted directly from the shifting balance of male to female births. Although the birth rate rose incredibly once the fertility system had been inaugurated, the sex of the great majority of the new children was female. Nine out of every ten were girls, and the proportion was still rising. Next year it might be ninety-two out of every hundred; the year after, ninety-four . . . And perhaps in the near, the too near, future, there would be no more boys. Only girls.

"Scientists and electronic brains worked intensively to discover the reason for this inexplicable disappearance of the male sex from the birth statistics. Some thought that Sterilin itself was acting as a sex-discriminating poison, acting through the female ovum to destroy any cell that might be fertilized by a twenty-three chromosome male gamete. But even the most sensitive tests failed to show that there was any foundation to this theory. Female ova, to exist at all, had to be entirely free from Sterilin. The slightest trace of the drug in the female endocrine system completely inhibited ovulation. And extensive tests failed to prove that there was any difference in reaction between male and female gametes to Sterilin—or any reaction at all, for that matter. Sterilin, being derived from estrogen, had no effect whatever on male cells.

"The true answer was much more subtle and less capable of conclusive proof. It was postulated by a Dr. Stenniger that the attenuation of the male statistic in birth figures was a blind reaction of nature to the mass Sterilin addiction of the human race. From nature's point of view almost the entire female half of the human species had become sterile. What was the obvious compensating action? Simply to produce more females to replace those who had lost their capacity to conceive, Dr. Stenniger insisted.

"The only evidence to support this hypothesis lay in old population records which seemed to show that after major world wars in former years, there had been an increase of male births, presumably to compensate for the large number of males destroyed as a result of war. In a similar way, Dr. Stenniger pointed out, nature was compensating now for what was, in the planetary sense, a mass destruction of the female component of the species.

"Stenniger's hypothesis was accepted slowly and reluctantly; but it was accepted. Nature, it was realized, is slow to act, slow to produce change, and the danger lay in the fact that such change, once established, might prove to be irreversible. Evolution is a one-way street, and, like entropy, never works backwards.

"The elimination of male births had taken some seventy years to accomplish. Even if nature were co-operative enough to reverse the process (supposing that Sterilin could be uni-

versally banned), it would presumably take another seventy
years to re-establish the male. But seventy years was a lifetime; it could witness the entire destruction of the human
race by lack of men.

"On Government instructions, scientists concentrated on
the study of sexual cytology within strictly specified terms of
reference. Their object was to produce, in the laboratory, a
normal fusion of male gamete and female ovum to produce a
living composite cell of forty-seven chromosomes, capable
of developing, given suitable gestative conditions, into a
male child. They failed. During more than two hundred
thousand fertilization tests not a single male embryo was produced, and, strangest thing of all, there was no detectable
reason why it should be so.

"They were working, of course, on a purely statistical
basis, assuming that any particular sample of male gametes
would contain equal numbers of cells with and without the
vital sex chromosome. Had they been able to separate these
two different types of cells, a more conclusive result could
have been obtained, but there was no way of differentiating
between the cells without first killing and staining them for
microscopic examination. Even so, such examination merely
confirmed that both types of gametes, with and without the
necessary sex chromosome, were present in equal proportion.
And yet the male-producing gametes persistently failed to
function. It was as if nature had decreed that henceforth only
gametes containing twenty-four chromosomes would be capable of fertilizing the female ovum. It was sterility in reverse, a vicious and uncontrollable reaction aroused by the
indiscriminate use of Sterilin on a world-wide scale.

"The governments of the planet took no steps to prohibit
the use of Sterilin. Apart from the undeniable fact that it
would have been impossible, it was clearly seen that such a
move would achieve nothing, for birth statistics would still
favor the female for decades and perhaps generations to

come. The immediate problem was that of racial survival. If
the male sex were to become extinct (as indeed it might),
how could the remaining female section of humanity propagate itself?

"The answer was obvious to scientists and government
alike. Research had to be directed towards a form of artificial
parthenogenesis—induced virgin birth. By the application of
suitable drugs, and perhaps radiological techniques, the un-
fertilized female ovum had to be persuaded to split into two
cells, and so start the inevitable chain reaction of embry-
onic growth, resulting in birth.

"There was one snag: parthenogenesis by its very nature
could produce only females. The process of doubling up from
a single ovum with its twenty-four chromosomes could not at
any stage produce a cell with the male factor of forty-seven.
If artificial parthenogenesis could be achieved, it would solve
the problem of survival, but not of sex. There would never
be another man in the world, not in a million years.

"Information of that type could not be released. The two
and a half billion inhabitants of earth could never be permitted to learn about the shadow that was falling across their
future. Social stability had to be preserved, and, fortuitous-
ly, the mechanism for preserving it already existed in the fertility centers, the State nurseries, the new social apparatus
which detached child from mother soon after birth with,
in the majority of cases, no further contact throughout life.
Women gave birth to children, then promptly forgot them.
Nobody discussed maternity; it had became a duty in law
and was an unpleasant subject rapidly approaching the level
of obscenity. The fertility centers were prisons, albeit pleasant enough, and inevitably a certain stigma became associated with the process of compulsory fertility. The subject
was not openly discussed, and so the preponderance of female
births escaped public notice. And of course the information

services, including the newspapers, merely followed governmental direction. The truth was in safekeeping."

"There you have it," Brad said. "That's as much as I've
been able to find out. Now I need official confirmation."

Rona yawned lightly. "Brad, I think you're too inquisitive.
Even if what you say is true, what good will it do to tell the
world? People are happy enough in their ignorance. Why
alarm them and cause social unrest? Government scientists
might find the answer to everything in . . . well .   . no
time at all."

"The principle is wrong, honey. The government is making consultation with electronic brains when it should be
consulting the people. If there's a crisis, let's share it. If this
is to be the end of man, or even of the human race, let's go
down with dignity, with the correct principles, and not in a
kind of neo-fascist, security-ridden condition of ruthless suppression. We have a right to know about our future, Rona—all
of us."

"The government doesn't share you're view, Brad."

"The government doesn't share anything. What about you?
Whose side are you on?"

She smiled and wriggled closer to him. "I'm on my own
side, darling. And that could be your side too. Look, it's late
and we've talked too much. Come and see me here tomorrow
evening around eight. I'll do my best for you."

He kissed her gently. "Thanks, honey. I knew I could
rely on you."

"Any friend of Lecia's is a friend of mine," she whispered
vaguely.

XII

THE next morning Brad Somer returned to his apartment at
the Waldorf. The night had been satisfactory, and if Rona ful-
filled her promise then his assignment would be over. The
story would be ready to break, and the world would know
the truth about Sterilin, about childbirth, about the future.
He sensed a certain abstract justice in the pattern of events.
Man had chosen the inviting license of Sterilin-protected
amorality, and nature had counterattacked, logically and
inevitably, subtly undermining the entire erotic structure of
contemporary society.

Women had chosen sterility in the interests of sexual freedom; nature had responded with a fine sense of irony by
eliminating the male sex, and thereby setting a time limit
on that freedom. The moral was difficult to define; Brad
wasn't even sure if there was a moral. But somehow the blind
scales of cosmic justice seemed to be exactly balanced.

Twenty minutes after reaching the Waldorf, he had a
visitor. The internal phone rang, and reception announced the
arrival of a certain Miss Lecia Tarrant. She came up to his
room, raven-haired, green-eyed, rose-complexioned, and a
little breathless. He kissed her briefly.

"I'm worried, Brad. I had to come. It's about Rona."

He regarded her questioningly. "She's all right, Lecia. I
spent the night with her, and I'll be seeing her again this
evening."

"That's just the point, Brad. Rona isn't here any more.
Yesterday she was transferred to a government training center
at Carlisle."

Brad's expression betrayed the disbelief of his mind.

"It's true," Lecia went on anxiously. "She telephoned me
late last night."

He crossed to the window and stared thoughtfully at the morning traffic four stories below. The sunshine was bright on the gray road surface. The rains of yesterday had disappeared without trace. He turned to her abruptly.

"Then who was the woman I talked to and slept with? She answered to the name of Rona. She behaved like I imagined Rona would behave. She promised co-operation."

"She couldn't have been Rona," Lecia said, lighting a cigarette with trembling fingers.

He crossed to a deep sloping chair and flopped into it wearily. "One of us must be wrong, Lecia. I was with Rona, yet you say she telephoned you from Carlisle. How can you be sure it was her?"

"How can *you*, Brad?"

"Let's start at the beginning, honey. First: Why should she be transferred so suddenly?"

"Because they found out—about me and you—about your plan to obtain information from her."

"*Who* found out?"

"Security people. They have methods. There are ways of listening over phone circuits even when the receiver is down. There are zone-focusing microphones so sensitive they can pick up whispered conversations behind brick walls."

"Okay, so what exactly did Rona have to say?"

Lecia inhaled deeply, allowing the spent smoke to drift gently from her parted lips. *A real doll*, Brad thought. *Nicer than Rona, but too familiar to him over the years to retain much fundamental attraction to him. There was no mistaking the worry in the lines of her face, though.*

"She couldn't say much, Brad. The phone line was probably being monitored. It seems she was called into the departmental supervisor's office yesterday morning and told she had been posted to number seven statistical training center at Carlisle. Three hours later she was in a gyrojet and on her way."

"But . . . can you be sure . . . ?"

She nodded mutely.

Brad lay back in his seat, surveying the beige ceiling without really seeing it. He was conscious of uneasiness squirming in his abdomen, a faint apprehension, a sense of betrayal, the chilling shadow of insecurity.

"What did Rona look like?" he asked presently.

She came over to him and produced a small color photograph from the pocket of her coat. He studied it thoughtfully. It was a head-and-shoulder profile portrait of a pretty auburn-haired girl, not unlike the Rona he had entertained the previous evening, but somehow younger and a little softer in the line of her eyes. Looking at the photograph he realized suddenly the comparative hardness of the girl he had spent the night with, the shrewd modeling of her features, and the predetermined atmosphere of her words and movements. The uneasiness within him expanded.

"Well?" Lecia enquired.

He returned the photograph, pursing his lips doubtfully. "This other girl was similar, near enough to deceive someone who had never met the real Rona. She dressed just how you said Rona dressed, even down to the come-and-get-me stockings."

"They don't miss any details, Brad."

"So what does it all mean? Are they gunning for me?"

"More than that; they've got you trapped already. And me too. Whatever you said to the fake Rona last night is on record. There would be a microphone in the room wired to a recorder at the nearest security office. If you said anything compromising . . ."

He laughed, abruptly and harshly. "That's the understatement of the year. I can see it now, how she drew me out, got me to explain to her how much I knew, what I was trying to find out . . . even the source of my information. Don't worry, Lecia, I didn't tell her that. Nobody is implicated apart from you and Rona—and myself."

She came closer to him and placed her hands gently on his shoulders.

"When you go to see her tonight, Brad, there'll be security men waiting for you. They'll arrest you. And that will be the end of Brad Somer. The world will never know what happened to you and no one will ever care, anyway, except me."

"Maybe you won't be around to care, either, Lecia."

Her voice whispered quietly into his ear. "I've got a plan, Brad. It's the only way of escape for both of us. Look . . ."

She fumbled in her pocket and produced a small wallet. Opening it she withdrew two pale green tickets.

"Airline reservations to America. I have a friend who works for Transplanetary Jet Services. One for you and one for me."

He accepted the ticket and scrutinized it briefly.

"Three o'clock this afternoon," he said. "That's quick."

"It may not be quick enough, Brad. There's no time to waste. Leave the hotel without delay. Disappear for a few hours. Do everything you can to shake off anyone who might be shadowing you. Then meet me at the airport just a few minutes before the flight."

"Okay," he said slowly. "I'll be there, Lecia."

She smiled pallidly and kissed him on the lips. "And keep your fingers crossed for both of us, darling."

She left soon after, and only the green airline reservation remained to recall the sudden menace she had brought into his life.

After Lecia had left the room Brad crossed to the window and gazed abstractedly down and out towards the road below. London was peaceful and quiet as yet. The morning was young and the flood tide of traffic and pedestrians was still building up. There was no hint of the sinister or the ominous in the outside world. The buildings were gray and solid, as they had been for many decades, and the people who moved about on the distant pavements were minute, animated dolls, quite ordinary and unremarkable.

Lecia could have been mistaken, though it did not seem very likely. She was too finely intelligent a woman to jump to a dramatically wrong conclusion without adequate motive, and yet, supposing her motive was different from what he had been led to believe? The airline reservations had been a little too pat—too contrived. They had followed too closely on the alarming exposure of his own danger.

Looking at the facts more leisurely, and he felt he had time to do just that, what was the net result of Lecia's visit? That he had been stampeded into accepting an unexpected airlift to America, and more, into taking Lecia with him. It began to add up. For a long time he had suspected that Lecia's emotional attachment towards him was stronger than the current code of amorous behavior considered delicate, and recently he had become aware of a certain restlessness in her attitude towards living. She wanted to move on, to move on with the man she loved, into the more glamorous world of hyper-civilized America, and away from the darkening, security-ridden environment of Britain. She was planning ahead, arranging the pattern of her own future, and using the dangers of the present-day, tightly controlled society to accelerate the fulfillment of her plans. For all he knew Rona, too, might be part of the plot.

He began to feel angry and resentful, and the anger was to some extent directed against his own blindness and stupidity. Men were becoming a rare commodity, and women everywhere were seeking to bind their men into a relationship that exceeded the requirements of modern male-female liaison. Lecia had been astute, but not quite astute enough. He smiled grimly to himself.

And then he saw her, far below, crossing the road outside the entrance to the hotel. He watched the tiny animated shape that was her, feeling remote and vaguely omnipotent, like some kind of all-seeing cynical god. She reached the opposite curb and began to walk towards the distant Underground station.

It happened so suddenly that he was taken completely by surprise. A long black car curved from the inner traffic lane and abruptly stopped ahead of Lecia. Like a movie run in rapid motion, two men emerged from the car and moved to either side of the girl. There seemed to be some kind of a struggle, and she seemed to fall. Next moment she was being dragged towards the car, and, in an instant, the car had moved off and was merging with the denser traffic filtering towards the Strand.

Astonishment petrified him for several seconds. His immediate reaction when the temporary paralysis had evaporated was to rush down into the road, seize the nearest taxi, and follow the car. But time was against him. He crossed to the phone and lifted it, intending to call the police, but replaced it slowly. An appalling thought had taken possession of his mind. *Lecia had been right He was trapped.*

He picked up the airline ticket from the table, holding it firmly, almost with desperation. The sense of betrayal that he had experienced earlier now held his mind in an inflexible grip, and the need for escape obsessed him No longer was there any need to obtain factual confirmation of his news story; Lecia's fate was confirmation enough. The world was at bay, and authority was intolerant of subversion even when it came in the form of truth.

Supposing, he thought, *supposing they interrogate her and discover what she had planned. Supposing they search her and find the other airline ticket. Supposing they are waiting for me at the airport . . .*

His brain recoiled from the torment of his suspicions, and he sought consolation in his knowledge of Lecia's regard for him. It might even be love; sometimes people did experience

the regressive emotion known as love, and when they were
so possessed they became fanatically loyal to the object of
their love . . . loyal to the point of death. She would destroy
the ticket, and she would not talk. Brad felt convinced of
that.

There was nothing he could do but pack, and leave as
quickly as possible. Time was running out and the deadline
was three o'clock.

The airport was busy, and the departure lounge was
crowded, for which Brad was immensely thankful. Mingling
with the masses of air travelers he felt safe, secluded, almost
protected. His flight number was four-two-three, he had
learned, and in a little over ten minutes he would be sitting
in the resilient bucket seat of the jetliner, rising swiftly into
the blue sky, towards safety and freedom.

He sat on a chair in an obscure corner of the lounge, reading a newspaper which he held high in front of his face. The
seconds ticked by silently in his mind, and he was aware of
each one as it passed. People moved around, ordinary people,
men and women, and even a few children, and the air vibrated with a score of mingled conversations.

Although the newspaper filled his field of vision, the head-
lines were meaningless to his agitated eyes. Occasionally he
glanced covertly above and around the sides of the paper,
scanning in brief darting glances the throng of people in the
lounge, seeking the face or the figure that would sound a stri-
dent alarm in his brain. But there were no tall sinister men
and no expressionless faces. He was one of a multitude of
lovely, and mostly happy, people awaiting the summons of
the loudspeaker to join their jetliner.

"Flight four . . . two-three," said the loudspeaker in crisp
impersonal tones. "Runway seven. Will passengers for this
flight kindly proceed to the departure point. Take off in seven
minutes."

He did not move immediately. It was wise to be neither
first nor last, but to remain one of the middle people, the
anonymous, unnoticed ones. Presently he folded his paper and
joined the throng of individuals converging on the door.

Beyond the door was the immense foyer, and beyond that
the glass doors opening on the airport itself, with its massive
runways intermeshed like the canals of Mars. A double-
decker coach was waiting outside the doors to convey the
passengers over the half mile of concrete to the departure
point where the giant jetliner waited in silent, powerful im-
patience.

A sense of freedom filtered into his mind, lightening his
step and adding a certain zest to his movements. He began to
whistle. The worst was over. Lecia had kept faith with him
There was nothing he could do about her now; one man
couldn't fight the immense closely integrated secret security
force of a powerful government Escape was the only solution.

He was halfway to the glass door when an arm gently
linked into his. His heart raced momentarily He forced
himself to look round.

Rona was walking beside him, smiling pleasantly. He didn't
dare stop. The glass door was only a dozen yards away.

"I'm surprised at you, Brad," Rona said quietly "I thought
you liked me, honestly I did."

He said nothing, but walked forward with urgent steps
She tugged at his arm.

"I never knew a guy in such a hurry. It's not very com-
plimentary, Brad. A girl has to study her own interests
these days."

He stopped abruptly, turning to face her, and fighting the
sudden fear that gnawed at his abdomen. Uncertainty undermined his resolve, uncertainty about her, uncertainty about
himself.

"Rona," he said, "I had a sudden recall. I have to get back

to the States on this flight. It's a personal matter . . ."

"It's more personal than you think," she replied softly.

Something glinted below eye level. Glancing down he saw distinctly the barrel of a small automatic pistol peering from her clenched fist. And then he became aware of two stationary figures standing like shadows behind her—gaunt, lean men with eyes of granite.

"Come with me, Brad," she said.

He looked once towards the glass door and the airline coach filling with passengers. It might have been a billion light years away. Without feeling or reaction he allowed her to take his arm again, this time with firmer fingers, and permitted himself to be guided obliquely across the foyer to a staircase.

It was a small office on the first floor, with a wide window overlooking the runways. The desk and the chairs wore a thin film of dust, and the room possessed an atmosphere of stagnation and desolation strangely out of keeping with the ultra-modern decor of the airport building. He was aware of a quality of disuse, of isolated privacy.

The gaunt men moved apart, one to the window and one to the door, and remained motionless, hands in pockets, eyeing him stonily. Only Rona remained friendly and warm, regarding him archly with a hint of veiled amusement. She was still holding the gun.

"For an honest man with nothing on his conscience you ask very few questions," she said. "Don't you want to know what this is all about?"

He shook his head slowly. His mind had already sealed itself off from the immediate present and was casting around for a line of action. The coach would be just about full now, ready to move off to the departure point. He had a minute, perhaps less. There was no time to talk or listen.

"I'm sorry it has to be this way, Brad," Rona went on. "The State rates security very highly, and as a servant of the

State it is my unpleasant duty to carry out its policy. I'm sorry it had to be you. I was beginning to develop a genuine affection for you."

A pause while she weighed the gun speculatively in her hand.

"Brad Somer, I am arresting you under the Emergency Regulations of the Social Stability Act for subversive activity contrary to internal security. I must ask you to accompany me to Security Headquarters."

The gaunt men began to close in on him. With each step they took he sensed his future diminishing and darkening. A brightly lucid thought illuminated his mind in an instant of self-criticism. Why did men facing certain death so often refrain from risking their lives? Inaction could achieve nothing: action could not achieve less, but it might secure an advantage.

He kicked her legs from under her with one vicious swing of his foot, then instantly flung himself on top of her and grappled for the gun. The men were flitting bat shadows on either side of him. The gun was in his hand and his finger was squeezing the trigger of its own volition. There was no sound, just the barely inaudible click of some internal mechanism and the faint sighing of displaced air as the slugs were hurled from their chambers. Dope slugs, he thought briefly, nonlethal, anaesthetic, but nonetheless effective.

It was all over before he realized it. Rona and the two men lay paralyzed and immobile on the floor, looking in some way strangely unreal, like a single frame from a slow-motion movie. His heart was pounding violently and his lungs were gasping for air, but there was no time to waste.

He slipped the dope pistol into his pocket then rushed from the room and down the stairs, almost throwing himself across the foyer towards the glass door. The coach was beginning to move. In one final, punishing effort he caught up with it and forced the door open. Helping hands seized him. A moment later he was lying almost prostrated in one of the deep resilient seats, and voices around him were talking.

"Gee, mister, you nearly didn't make it."

"How come you didn't hear the flight warning?"

"That was some run, friend. World record I'd say . . ."

He didn't care. The past had suddenly slipped away from him, and the future was warm and welcoming.

The jetliner took off dead on time, and ascended rapidly to thirty-thousand feet, where it leaped forward on booster jets and broke through the sound barrier without sound or vibration. Twenty minutes later, when the automatic pilot took over, the aircraft was cruising at a steady 3,500 knots.

Brad sat slumped in his window seat, lost in a kind of thought that didn't involve thinking, staring out at the white cloud masses far below. Facing the tail, he was aware that the sun was on his right, casting shadows across the features of his fellow passengers almost opposite.

He recognized his lack of emotion as a symptom of psychological shock. Too many things had happened in too short a time. It was one thing to be a roving journalist in pursuit of facts, but it was quite another thing to be the pursued, to find yourself suddenly and unwittingly the victim of ruthlessly applied security. To witness the sudden disintegration of people you knew: Rona, the real Rona, then Lecia, and to find the web of intrigue spread all around you, was to realize abruptly the sinister strength of the shadow you were investigating and to appreciate fully the true nature of its power. In the long run, when it came to the point, personal life always seemed more important than the threat of universal death.

It was over now. There might be trouble with security in America, but it would only be trouble. He felt that the American government didn't take the problem of concealing the gradual elimination of the male sex quite so seriously as in Britain. Perhaps it was because the U.S.A. had always been dominated by women, and men had always played a somewhat subordinate part in the social structure; but that was just a glib theory, he knew.

In less than one hour he would be back on his native soil, able to breathe freely and able to think again with a mind uninhibited and unconstricted by fear and apprehension. And he had the story now, with enough confirmation to give it strength, ready to break on an unsuspecting world. The scoop of all time—the story of mass male suicide.

After a while it came to him that the sunlight filtering through the cabin windows had moved, though he was unable at first to define exactly how. But presently he realized that, curiously, the sun was no longer on his right, but was shining from the left. Unable to comprehend this unexpected change of orientation he peered through the window, attempting to make sense from nonsense.

His mind, seeking some intelligible clue, suddenly focused itself on the background of murmured conversation in the cabin. He became aware of a certain subdued excitement in the voices around him. One voice particularly, an aggressive American voice, demanded: "Why the hell have we turned back?"

Turned back . . . The phrase reverberated hollowly in the cavity of his skull. He stared incredulously out of the window towards the sun, and saw only confirmation of his fears. The jetliner had indeed turned back.

The reason was not far to seek. Security had played its next move. The aircraft had not yet reached the point of no return and was still under the control of the United Kingdom navigation network. An authoritative order from the ground to turn back would have to be obeyed.

And they would be waiting for him at the airport, and this time there would be no mistake . . .

He bit his lower lip and looked around. At the far end of the cabin, near the door to the flight deck, a cluster of passengers were excitedly interrogating the air hostess. Fragments of question and answer came to his ears. *There is no cause for alarm, sir . . . But I have an appointment in New York in just over an hour . . . What's the trouble, miss; is it weather? . . . We have to carry out ground network instructions, sir . . . I wanna talk to the captain; I insist on talking to the captain . . .*

The captain, thought Brad. *He was the key to the situation!* He slipped one hand stealthily into his pocket and stroked the cold, reassuring shape of the dope pistol.

Slowly he stood up and joined the group near the flight deck door. A moment or two of hesitation, of cautious maneuvering for position, and then he had achieved his purpose. He closed the flight deck door silently behind him.

The navigator glanced up inquisitively from his plotting table and murmured something into the intercom microphone. The radio officer abandoned the controls of his equipment and swung round on his swivel chair. There was no hostility in their expressions, just curiosity.

Brad produced the gun and the atmosphere changed instantly. The other men became tense, guarded and uncertain of themselves, knowing they would have to react, but not quite sure how.

"No tricks," Brad said coldly. "I mean business."

He pointed to the radio officer. "Shut down your equipment."

"Are you crazy? We can't land without radio."

"We're not landing—not yet awhile. Shut it down." He pointed the gun at the navigator. "Radar too."

They didn't move. He aimed the gun at a glowing amber radar screen.

"Shut it down before I wreck it."

There was no mistaking the stubborn defiance in the navigator's eyes. Brad squeezed the trigger. The dope slug in its soluble skin was by no means armor-piercing, but it was capable of shattering glass. The radar tube imploded abruptly, spraying fine glittering shards of glass over the plotting table.

"You bloody maniac!" shouted the navigator, switching off the equipment.

Brad turned his attention to the radio officer. In a moment the shrill noise of the radio power unit whined into silence as the switches were opened. The two men stared sullenly at him.

"Don't move," said Brad, "and don't leave the flight deck. It would be foolish to alarm the passengers."

Watching both men carefully he crossed to the control cabin and opened the communicating door. The pilot was sitting well back in his seat, smoking a cigarette and shaking the ash over the small, carpeted floorspace. The copilot was staring out over the ocean, propping his chin in his hands, in a posture that suggested boredom.

Brad tapped the pilot on the head with the barrel of his gun. The man swung round peevishly, but froze immediately as his eyes focused on the weapon He looked starkly into Brad's face.

The copilot, sensing the movement, turned his head, registered alarm for an instant, then struggled to get out of his seat. Brad pushed him gently back again.

"Turn round," he ordered, but they didn't understand his meaning.

"There's been a change of plan," he stated, speaking slowly and distinctly above the pervading throb of the jets "We're going on to New York after all. So turn her around—quickly!"

The pilot shook his head. "Nothing doing. Better put that gun away before you do some damage. There are forty passengers on this craft."

"I know, and I don't care. If you go back to London I die automatically in a few hours, a few days. If I destroy this aircraft I die a little sooner, that's all. If I reach America I live. It's as simple as that."

"Tell it to the police when we land," said the pilot.

Brad took a deep breath and gripped the gun more firmly. "Turn her around—now!"

The pilot turned to face the controls, then folded his arms. "Go to hell," he said firmly.

Brad shot him in the back. The dope slug made a tiny hole in his tunic and blood glistened for a few moments, then clotted rapidly as the slug dissolved in the warm flesh. The anaesthetic effect was almost instantaneous. The pilot stiffened abruptly, made to push himself erect, then collapsed across the seat, his right arm dangling limply close to the undercarriage control levers. The unconsciousness would last for about an hour.

The copilot was staring at his partner as if unable to believe his eyes. Brad concentrated his attention on him.

"Turn her around," he said firmly.

Rebellion flared briefly in the other man's eyes. He was older than his colleague, Brad observed, possibly a family man, with a wife and children waiting for him back home. There was even something homely in the brown of his eyes and the clipped softness of his graying mustache. He wouldn't want to flirt with death too much . . .

"Turn her around," Brad repeated.

The copilot hesitated, shrugged his shoulders, then took over control of the jetliner. Presently the horizon ahead tilted slowly and the sun swung around in a vast arc and the Atlantic Ocean below reversed itself: the aircraft was once again pointing towards the west.

Brad remained on the flight deck, taking up a position by the pilot's communicating door so that he could supervise the copilot and keep a watchful eye on the other members of the crew to his rear. From where he was standing he could not clearly see the radio officer, and it seemed to him at one time that the man was manipulating the communications equipment, perhaps contacting the ground network to inform them of the dramatic events that had occurred. It didn't matter. America was the destination, and he would be able to justify the violent line he had taken. The press would back him up, and clever lawyers would twist the law to exonerate him. There was nothing to worry about.

In a day or two he would explode the bombshell that would startle the entire world. At first they would not believe him, but independent authorities would begin to check the statistics and make computations, and gradually they would know the truth, the truth that he had slowly and methodically ferreted out in defiance of suppression and censorship and security. The news of the approaching death of mankind.

Becoming engrossed in his thoughts he did not observe the five black specks approaching from high in the northern sky until they were quite close. Puzzled, he leaned over the unconscious pilot to see them better. They were aircraft of some kind, small and swift, with delta wings and large in-line jets. *Rather like high-speed military fighters,* he thought uncomfortably.

The copilot had noticed them too. He glanced quickly at Brad, frowning a little, and there was something vaguely disquieting in his expression. He pulled back on the control column so that the jetliner began to climb gently.

The fighter planes made a complete circle, closing in all the time. It was now possible to see the pilots silhouetted in their sealed control turrets; they looked black and sinister. The planes swept away in a wide ellipse, then came back again, and this time they were very close. Brad saw that they were painted jet black and bore no identification markings.

Uneasiness began to twist blindly in his abdomen. The fighters flashed past, reappearing after a few seconds on the other side, and then, as if in synchronism, turned and bore down on the jetliner. The delta wings flashed orange. Incandescent fingers struck rapidly through space. A moment later the jetliner was aflame throughout its length as incendiary rockets exploded within its fuselage.

In consternation Brad gripped the back of the pilot's seat, paralyzed beyond all thought or feeling. The aircraft shook with subdued thunder, and looking through the starboard window he saw that one wing was alight in brilliant amber flame that belched a streamer of _dense black smoke behind it. The copilot struggled insanely with the controls, his face ashen.

It seemed to Brad that the ocean far below tilted slowly upwards until it blotted out the sky, and the throb of the jets was drowned by a new terrifying sound—a tearing, shrieking sound of air being torn apart by a plunging mass of metal. In the intensity of his personal horror he did not even hear the screams that filtered from the passenger compartment.

Seconds remained, and he knew it. No time to think—no time to plan—no time to do anything but stare in frantic disbelief at the immense green wall of water rushing upwards at incredible speed. But somewhere at the back of his mind he knew that he had lost the battle. They had achieved checkmate and won the game. The deaths of nearly a hundred other people, passengers and crew, were unimportant— *they had destroyed him, Brad Somer, and had preserved their secret.*

It was the beginning of the end, he realized; not for himself or the other terrified people in the aircraft, but for the whole human race! This plane contained death of freedom and the individual, and the birth of a new kind of despotism acting under the guise of security.

When the jetliner hit the ocean it was still traveling faster than sound. Nothing remained. Nothing.

PART FOUR

THE PATRIARCH

XIII

ON HIS seventy-fifth birthday Old Gavor was presented with a massive birthday cake bearing seventy-five electronic candles. The candles were so triggered that, at the slightest puff of breath from Gavor's feeble and wrinkled lips, they extinguished themselves automatically and in precise sequence, spelling out in dark ephemeral lines the words "Happy Birthday." It was a welcome touch of sentiment in a world that had long abandoned any pretension to sentiment. It was a gimmick designed to keep the last man in a childishly contented frame of mind, and Old Gavor knew it, but he didn't care any more.

For most of the day he amused himself by blowing out the electronic candles over and over again; the novelty remained fresh with him until late in the evening. Then he began to tire, and with the fatigue came peevishness. He took a knife and attempted to cut the cake in half, but, of course, it was made from a polythene compound and inedible, and presently, frustrated and annoyed, he swept the thing from the table on to the luxuriously carpeted floor, where it flashed and sparked and sputtered for several seconds, then emitted blue smoke as it lay dead and distorted.

Sulkily he crossed to the door and pressed the fourth button down on the adjacent control panel. A green light winked merrily. He scowled irascibly, then returned to the polythene cake on the floor and kicked it viciously. It flashed and belched more smoke, then became inanimate.

A moment later the door opened and a young woman entered. She was dark and olive complexioned, with deep brown eyes in which sincerity seemed mingled with a hint of the sardonic. Her dress was brief, in a translucent green, and her legs (which were the principle focus of Old Gavor's glazed eyes) were of satin pink.

She looked at the damaged polythene cake, then at the old man, and shook her head sorrowfully, but with a glint of humor in her eyes. "You're a naughty boy, Gavor," she said in mild reproof. "You could be reprimanded for this."

She picked up the cake and replaced it on the table.

"I'm fed up," Old Gavor complained in his reedy voice. "All you give me are toys to play with. I'm tired of toys. I want to get around, to see the world. I'm old enough, aren't I?"

The girl smiled. "The world is a big place and it is full of women. You wouldn't be safe."

Old Gavor snorted. "I have been a prisoner in this building for more than a generation. I want freedom. I want my rights."

"You haven't any rights," said the girl pleasantly. "You're State property and we have to take good care of you."

"I can take care of myself. I want to get out and walk the streets of London before I die."

"The streets of London are crowded, and dangerous for an old man. You can see them on television."

"Damn television! Damn you all. I'd rather die. I want to die. Tell your Mistress that."

The girl took his arms and eased him gently into a chair. "Now you're being antisocial. You still have a duty towards society. Remember, you are the last man. Once you are dead we no longer have a source of male gametes for our laboratory experiments."

"I'm a guinea pig; that's what I am."

"Not at all, Gavor. Rather, let us say, you are a culture from which we can obtain certain unique micro-organisms that may help to save the world."

Old Gavor spat angrily on the floor. "I don't want to be a culture. I want to be let alone, to get around, to see things and people."

"There are no people any more, only women. And don't spit, it's unhygienic."

Old Gavor growled in his beard. The beard was quite unkempt, and covered his face like a miniature undergrowth, from which only his bright blue eyes and his long shiny nose peeped almost apologetically. Despite his age he was sprightly enough, but his sprightliness possessed a brittle, enfeebled quality which was reflected in the bony structure of his wrists and his skeletal hands. He was dressed conventionally in a suit of dark gray, shiny at the seat and elbows. New clothes were available to him at a snap of the fingers, but he preferred the untidy comfort of those he had worn for years.

"You're like an old horse," the girl explained, "set to graze in the twilight of its life. You've had your day and had your fun."

The old man chuckled abruptly. "How many did I have? Ten thousand, twenty thousand . . . ?"

"More. Nearly thirty thousand children in all, including those produced in incubators. And every one a girl."

"Not bad, eh? And I'm not finished yet."

"By no means. The incubators are still breeding your progeny. Who knows, one might be a boy. That would change the course of history."

"I wasn't thinking of incubators," said Gavor scowling. "I meant like in the old days. Why don't I have women to stay with me now?"

The girl smiled. "At seventy-five? Besides, it's wasteful. We have more efficient methods."

Old Gavor grunted in disgust. "Glass tubes and machinery. I don't like it. Besides, I'm not so old as I look. Once in a while I'd like to . . ."

"I'll speak to the Mistress about it, but it's not quite so simple as you think. There have been changes in society during the past generation. Very few of the mature women of today remember men at all, and they accept the world of women as normal. Women are born into a matriarchy, and, if anything, they look upon men as obsolete freaks of nature."

"Bah!" Gavor breathed indignantly. "You send them in to me. I'll show them who's a freak."

"It is a matter of basic psychology. When you have women living together without men, there has to be some kind of emotional outlet which is independent of the male sex. In other words, Gavor, the society you are living in is rapidly becoming homosexual; but in the nicest possible way."

"Bah!" Gavor repeated.

"The truth is that there are very few women alive today who would not be repelled by the thought of having relations with a man, with you, for instance. And those who are old enough to remember, and preserve something of their formed heterosexual mentality, have already passed the climacteric. They are not eager."

"What about you? You're a likely girl."

"I am as the others—a Lesbian."

"You ought to be ashamed to admit it."

"Shame died a natural death when Sterilin was invented. We have to adapt ourselves to the new conditions of living as best we can."

"Well, Lesbian or not, you could do an old man a good turn."

She smiled sardonically. "I should be exceeding my terms of reference. All I can do for you is to prescribe a bromide."

"To hell with your bromide." He stood up suddenly and

grasped her arms with hard, bony fingers. "You're supposed to look after me, give me what I want . . ."

She twisted her arms from his senile grip with a lithe flexing movement. "Don't be an old fool, Gavor. You're living in a past that died a long time ago. I'm a tolerant woman, but not *that* tolerant." She pushed him back into his chair. "Sit down and cool off. You should be making your plans for the next world, instead of getting intoxicated on your gonadotropic hormones. Women are different nowadays, and the sooner you realize it the better. They think differently and behave differently. The basic things of life are different. Men are no longer necessary, and women don't miss them."

Old Gavor attempted to sneer, but his beard concealed the twist of his lips. "How about the next generation? Incubators won't help you there . . ."

"We don't use incubators, other than for experimental work in embryology. The next generation is assured Scientists discovered the secret of parthenogenesis many years ago. We can produce the next generation to order, by drugs and radiation."

"It's not natural. It won't work forever."

"We don't rely on nature any more; science is more reliable. And parthenogensis works, and will go on working for five thousand years—ten thousand—a hundred thousand."

"But only girls."

"Of course. That's the beauty of it, the simple basic economy. Parthenogenesis can only produce females. And those females can only produce more females. There will never again be another natural male birth unless we can create a male embryo artificially in the laboratory. And that seems unlikely."

"I don't like your world," Old Gavor said sadly. "It is cold and inhuman. All those women having drugs and radiation, without love, without any kind of human relationship . . ."

"Stop feeling frustrated and sorry for yourself, Gavor. The women are happy enough. You see, they don't know about the drugs and the radiation. That is a State secret known only to a limited number of State officials. The great majority of women in the world believe that parthenogenesis is natural, a modern miracle of nature to compensate for the disappearance of man. They marvel at it. They delight in it."

"So you don't even stop at deception . . ."

"The truth is not always politic. Society is in the process of adapting itself to new conditions of living. We in authority must do our best to help the adaptation along: a white lie here, a little merciful distortion there, and a little general enforcement of overall policy . . ."

"Like encouraging Lesbianism . . . ?"

"That is only one factor among many. In a way you are privileged, Gavor. You have lived long enough to witness the birth of a new era in human affairs, the creation of a completely different society, a new kind of world. When you die history will start again for a new humanity of only one sex. We are trying to plan ahead, to anticipate the social forces that will operate in the years to come, and to legislate for them.'

Old Gavor shook his head slowly. "You are using words an old man doesn't understand. I'm tired. I don't want to hear any more."

"That's better," the girl said gently. "You've had a tiring day and it's getting late. Time you thought about going to bed."

Old Gavor regarded her sulkily. "I should have thought that on my birthday, at least . . ."

"I promise that I'll mention it to the Mistress. She may be able to find a volunteer, but it will take time. Well, goodnight, Gavor."

He didn't bother to reply. She left the room quietly. He was only conscious of the offensive words that echoed and

re-echoed in his brain: *She may be able to find a volunteer*
. . .

If I am the last man, then I ought to be king of the world,
Gavor told himself in a mood of childish resentment. I ought
to be the patriarch. A little tin god with unlimited power. But
what am I really? Just an old man confined to a suite of
rooms. I'm a prisoner, and I can't even be sure that I *am* the
last man. I only know what they tell me. It may be lies.
There may be other men, too, men who are also prisoners
These new women have their own standards of conduct.
Ethics I don't even begin to understand.

Why, only twenty years ago there were at least four thousand men in the State Male Reservation. Those were the good
days. Before the scientists got to work on this parthenogenesis business, when men were still necessary, and when the
few remaining ones were stallions in a stud, with nothing to
do but keep the birth statistics from falling to zero. And all
the time the women were waiting and praying for the birth
of a male child, as if it were some kind of second Messiah
But it never happened. Once nature starts something, she
never lets up.

And yet it was then that the trouble started, when we men
allowed ourselves to be rounded up and used as a kind of
fertility machine. We could have been masters of the situation. Instead we lived from day to day, telling ourselves that
what we were doing was a solemn duty for the sake of a
dying humanity, and we allowed the women to take control.

We did not foresee that the State Male Reservation was
the first step in the establishment of the new kind of society.
Science had solved the problem of survival, and induced
parthenogenesis had arrived. The sociologists and psychologists were already at work visualizing the structure of the
coming world without men. The foundations had to be laid.

They're strange, these modern women. They're cold, hard,
utterly without sentiment. Their brains think dispassionately,

just like the electronic computors they use to assist their planning. Why, one of these days they may even build a big electronic computing engine to do their thinking for them.

They remind me of a fanatical political group, single-minded, purposeful, with a particular goal in mind, never deviating from the path assigned by the scientists and social statisticians. They're women who want to be robots because they think that being robots is going to solve all their problems.

When parthenogenesis came, humanity found that it could survive on a monosexual basis. That meant a drastic change in habits and behavior. A new kind of neurotic living had to begin, and begin as quickly as possible. So they rounded us up, we men, and kept using us to serve the women they selected, hoping for the one male birth that could save the situation. We were an isolated unit, cut off from the world outside, and the world knew only what the government information services chose to release. We had disappeared, and the world assumed, in time, that man was extinct. The new parthenogenetic age could go ahead as planned.

And when, after many years, some of the remaining men grew restless and began to demand their liberty, they split us up. We were dispersed throughout the world, each man assigned to work in conjunction with a particular laboratory, to aid in the search for a living male embryo. That was the last I ever saw of any man. They may be dead, or some may still live. They tell me I'm the last man, and perhaps they tell the others the same? Why? To make us feel privileged? To make us feel helpless? That nothing we may do can matter any more?

Even the natural functions are denied, and have been for years. Science has replaced the concubine with the injection, the light anaesthetic, the glass tubes and the glittering equipment. They take what they want, and in return they provide shelter, food, and electronic toys like television and polythene cakes with automatic winking candles.

What is going on in the world outside? What are the women doing with the civilization that man created? They give me hints and broad outlines, but how much of it is true? Selective science, for instance: the canalizing of research into functional projects. No more unprofitable ventures into high speed flight or rockets into space. The world itself is waiting to be developed. The sciences of atomics and electronics must be applied in the service of humanity and the State. The frontiers of science will only be assailed when the knowledge so gained can be usefully applied for the direct benefit of society of this planet. Science is no longer the pursuit of knowledge for its own sake; it has become an instrument of the State, designed to improve and strengthen the machinery of the State. One more step towards the human anthill, perhaps . . .

I'm seventy-five today I'm an old man, though I don't feel a day over sixty. There can't be long to go for me, and I've nothing to lose any more. Just to look around, that's all I ask. To break loose for a while and be free. I keep asking, but they give evasive answers. But I've nothing to lose if I force the issue. They can't kill me while I can still produce what they want for their incubators and test tubes, and even if they do, well, death isn't so very far away in any case.

I'll do it. Tonight. Now.

XIV

EXACTLY what it was he intended to do, Old Gavor would have been hard put to define. There was an urgency in his mind that had to be relieved on a tactical basis, for there was no way of thinking ahead He knew nothing of the building in which he had lived for more years than he cared to remember. His entire world consisted of four air-conditioned, thermostatically heated rooms, comfortably furnished, and the usual toilet accessories. He had never explored beyond the heavy roller door at the end of the corridor. Nor did he know whether his apartment was above or below ground level, for there were no windows to guide him.

Escape, in the first instance, was a simple matter of getting beyond the roller door, which was always kept locked from the outside. It was opened only when one of his attendants entered or left the apartment, at his summons, or to bring him food and drink. The door, which seemed to be electrically operated, would roll back, remain stationary for about four seconds, then quickly close again. That was his only avenue of escape.

His mind pecked at the problem alertly, in a superficial, birdlike way. Ordinarily there could be no chance of his rushing the door as the attendant entered or left, for the women assigned to look after him were strong and well-versed in the art of self-defense. The solution to the problem would obviously have to be a violent one.

He picked up a chair, weighing it speculatively in his hands. The thing was made of chrome tube and flexible plastic; it was light, easy to swing, but hard enough to serve as a weapon.

He carried the chair down the short corridor to the roller door, then, leaving it there, returned to his room and pressed a wall button. Immediately he returned to the roller door and picked up the chair, holding it above his head, hands tightly clenched on the chrome tubing of the back.

A brief eternity seemed to pass before the door began to move. Old Gavor took a deep breath and waited. In a moment the door was open and the dark, olive skinned girl was looking at him with startled eyes. He hesitated no longer, but swung the chair downwards with all the force his frail muscles could exert. The sound of the blow was sickening.

One instant the girl was standing there; next instant she was a crumpled shape on the floor.

Dropping the chair, he seized her arms and dragged her into the corridor. Exultation bubbled within him. The girl was unconscious, the door was open, and there was nothing to prevent his escape.

Except the chair. Forgetting about it momentarily in the exertion of the moment, he stepped backwards after moving the girl. His foot struck something, and a hard shape poked into the back of his knees. He went over with a crash, his legs tangled in chrome tube and plastic.

Cursing luridly he pushed himself to his feet, holding an injured shoulder, and threw himself towards the door. He was a fraction too late. Within inches of it he was dismayed to see the gleaming wall of metal glide swiftly across the opening with scarcely a sound.

Angry and frustrated he glared at the door, then beat upon its cold hard surface with his bare hands. There were no indentations, no cavities, no sign of a concealed keyhole. The door was impregnable.

On the other hand, there had to be a way of opening it from the inside. The attendants could do it, though he had never learned how. Perhaps some electronic device, a hidden transmitter concealed in their clothing, transmitting an impulse signal at the touch of a button. The girl was still unconscious, so there was time to find out.

Hurriedly with trembling fingers he patted the brief clothing she wore, but could feel nothing beyond the soft shape of her body underneath. His hands began to linger a little. And then he came across the belt.

It was beneath her dress, apparently clipped round her waist. He could follow the shape of it with his fingers, and it seemed to him to be thicker than a belt might reasonably be expected to be, and on its surface he could feel the protruding discs of buttons.

In triumph he flung back the dress, exposing the lower part of her body. The belt was of some flexible metal, blue-gray in color, and on either side of the center clip were four silver pushbuttons. Excitement possessed him; he might be old, but he was no fool when it came to the point.

He struggled with the clip to release the belt, but it refused to open. Baffled for a moment he stared at it, then realized abruptly that he was wasting time. All that was necessary was to press the right button, and the door would open —but *which* button?

As he sat reflectively, making up his mind, the girl stirred, just a spasmodic movement of one leg, and suddenly the belt did not seem to matter any more. Until she moved she had been a body, but with the movement came a sense of animation, of life, and she became a woman. Something mischievous began to jig about in his brain. He was an old man, was he? Well, he could show them just how old he was. There was plenty of life in the old skeleton yet.

I'll press the button later, he thought. There's no hurry. I can afford to wait a few minutes.

The act of rape proved to be more difficult than he had imagined, and he realized that he was old, after all—very old. But he persevered in a mood of aggressive stubbornness, and presently he felt ashamed of himself.

He pressed the silver buttons one by one. At the fifth contact the roller door opened.

He was in a corridor without windows, mellowly lit by a luminous ceiling. It curved on either side to vanishing point, and was level. It might have been high in the air or deep beneath the ground; there was no way of knowing. In one direction or the other lay escape: it might have been one hundred feet away, or one thousand yards. There might have been a staircase, or an elevator, or a pneumatic drop shaft, or a spiral incline. It was all in the future, and in some curious way time and space became intermingled, for each step forward was a second in time, and the seconds and distance merged so that the two were no longer independent. He counted the seconds and he counted the footsteps, and behind all was the rhythm of his own heartbeat, counting off the moments to release or annihilation.

The building was deserted, it seemed, and he came upon a staircase leading to an upper level. He ascended cautiously, flexing his ankles to avoid making any sound. Another corridor, another flight of stairs, but he kept ascending. And presently there were no more stairs, and the corridor he was in was a cul-de-sac. There were doors, four of them, in the corridor, but they were of the metal roller type, and there was no way of opening them. If he had had the patience and common sense to remove the electronic belt from the olive-skinned girl he raped not so long ago, he would have been able to open the doors. Perhaps behind those doors were the other last men of the world, sealed away forever until the liberating moment of death.

There was no time to pause and worry about them, if indeed they existed at all. Time was running out. The olive-skinned girl might be conscious by now, or she might be missed. At any moment the alarm might be raised. Escape became a precision operation, a matter of split second timing, difficult enough when you are seventy-five.

This must be the top, for there were no more stairs, and no elevators. There was nothing left but to descend, as quickly as possible on feeble legs. Four flights, five, six and seven. And still the building was deserted. Could it be that there was only one woman in the entire structure? But no, for he had seen several different faces, three or four, and there was also the Mistress in charge. In charge of what? A prison of some kind? How large or how small a staff would be required to run such an establishment?

There was no answer to his question, and the building

remained silent. Perhaps they thought escape was impossible, or unlikely. Perhaps they believed the prisoners would prefer the austere comfort of their apartment cells to what lay outside. Perhaps the outside world had become so alien that no man would voluntarily seek to escape into it?

There could be no turning back. He had committed a criminal act by any code of conduct, and the need for escape became more pressing as each second ticked by. But where *was* the outside world? How could he locate it in a tall building of windowless corridors and stairs, with uniform temperature and illumination so that each level was identical with the one above and the one below?

Descend. Quickly at first, then more slowly, for he was still an old man, and his energy had been drained by rape. Level after level of steel, metal, and plastic curving corridors and roller doors, featureless, identical, with no humanity, faced him. Perhaps he was now descending below ground level. Any one door might be the exit to the outside world, but there was no way of opening it. He had exchanged one prison for another. There was no escape, and he could no longer remember the location of his own apartment; it was lost in the maze of levels and corridors and doors.

After an hour he began to tire, and he sat on a stair to think. He remembered, with a certain sense of irony, that at no time had any special precautions been taken to prevent violent escape. The female attendants had always been unarmed and vulnerable. Presently the reason permeated his brain: escape was impossible. The building was a maze, a rat trap, a geometrical structure without form or orientation. The roller doors in the corridors might well have been fakes for all he knew. Perhaps there was only one apartment: the one he vacated an eternity ago, and perhaps all the rest was an elaborate facade designed to deceive you. Perhaps the building was designed to tire the would-be escaper, to disillusion him and destroy his spirit. In an old man that would not be so difficult to accomplish.

He continued to stumble down the stairs, rapidly losing faith and enthusiasm. It must have been the fourteenth or fifteenth level, above or below ground he did not know, but he still was descending. It might be that as he was descending the levels were moving upwards in some kind of infernal squirrel cage, so that he would descend forevermore. At the twentieth level of descent he stopped. There was no exit. Escape had become an abstraction with no roots in reality. Worse still, there was no way of finding his way back to his own apartment.

And still the stairs went down, falling endlessly into a kind of bottomless pit, spiraling eternally into the abyss. He realized that he was a fool, an old fool. Why didn't he stay in his comfortable apartment and take life as it came? Why worry about the outside world when you were seventy-five? Surely it was enough to survive and be looked after by pretty girls.

There must be somebody in the building—the Mistress, the attendants. Without them he could wander forever up and down the stairs and along the silent corridors. He could thirst and starve to death in desolate isolation, surrounded by closed doors. There was nothing left to do but appeal for help. He shouted louder and louder, until presently he realized in horror that he was screaming . . .

She came suddenly, perhaps minutes, perhaps hours, after he had abandoned all hope. She was the olive-skinned girl he raped a thousand years ago. Her face was a mask, a beautiful mask, and there was no feeling or emotion in her eyes. He pushed himself erect, feeling more like an animal than a human being. She stood on a higher stair, somehow remote and on another plane of being. Her eyes were steady and he could not face them . . .

"So you wanted to escape," said the girl. Her voice was calm, without rancor or hate.

"Yes," Old Gavor sighed. "I had that idea. I thought it would be easy. I didn't realize . . ."

"There are many things you do not realize, old man. You are out of touch with reality."

He hesitated. "Death is very close to me. Right and wrong have lost their meaning. There are things I want to do . . ."

"And things you have done."

He sensed the implication of her words, and nodded humbly. "I'm sorry . . ."

"Sorrow is meaningless. What is done is done. You sought escape and you shall have escape."

"I am no longer sure that I want it."

"We are just. You shall have what you sought. Follow me."

She turned and ascended the stairs. He followed her mechanically, stumbling over the steps, forcing himself upwards in defiance of the paralyzing weariness that was creeping into his limbs. He felt cold and shivery, as if *rigor mortis* were invading the fibre of his body.

Two flights, three flights, he ascended, and suddenly they were facing a roller door in a corridor. She turned to him, and he thought he could detect an element of sadness in her eyes.

"You will not be the first to pass through this door," she said, "and you will not be the last. Men do not vary. Even unto death they seek to enlarge their horizons, they seek escape. I shall not stop you now. Escape if you wish."

Her fingers touched her waist, pressing a concealed button on the unseen belt. The door rolled aside. Old Gavor remained motionless.

"Go," she ordered.

He hesitated. "Tell me: am I the last man?"

There was a ghost of a smile on her lips. "You are what

you are, Gavor. Once you are dead there will be neither men nor women on Earth. Now go."

Old Gavor walked into the corridor beyond the door and into the world.

The corridor was long and dark, and as he walked along it the air grew progressively colder. Old Gavor shivered in his sombre gray clothes. But there was a faint glow of light on the walls ahead, and he hurried towards it on his stumbling legs.

The glow became brighter and the cold became more intense, and presently the corridor came to an end. He was in the open, under a sky of midnight blue, with an immense crimson sun lying low on the horizon. Something flickered and undulated above him, and in a brief glance he observed the intermittent luminous curtains of aurora. The air howled with wind, and the ground was white with snow and ice. His breath frosted as it left his lips.

For fully a minute he stood motionless, surveying the wasteland, aware of the biting sting of cold in his flesh and bones. There was nothing on the immense white wilderness before him. It might have been a plateau in Antarctica, some bleak expanse of subzero landscape devoid of life and hope. The midnight sun glimmered dully; it was the color of blood.

He turned towards the corridor, but it was already sealed. The gleaming width of a metal door stared blankly at him. Above and on all sides the building towered—solid, cylindrical, with no light, but reflecting the dark red glow of the polar sun from its rounded concrete surface.

Many things became clear to Old Gavor. This was the prison, a citadel in a remote frigid corner of the world. This was the last abode of man, the final sepulchre of the male sex. The freezing wind whined in his ears and plucked at his clothes, paralyzing his body with every gust. He hammered on the door and screamed against the noise of the elements, but his voice was drowned in the tumult of nature.

How many men, he wondered, have perished this way—seeking freedom? How many have sought civilization, only to find raw nature? How many frozen bodies are out there in the snow and ice, dreaming the blank dreams of death while, thousands of miles away, the world they knew has reshaped itself and forgotten about them and their kind.

He hammered and screamed, but the door remained closed, and in the course of time the cold became gentle, and transformed itself into sleep. Acting on some unguessable instinct he moved off into the snow, away from the building, towards the crimson sun, seeking privacy for the final intimate act of his life, the release of life and the acceptance of death.

If I am the last man, he thought, *then this is indeed a moment of history.*

Within the hour his body was buried beneath inches of snow, and the blood in his veins had crystallised into scarlet ice.

PART FIVE

THE CHILD

XV

AN EVENT of major importance had occurred in biophysical laboratory number five. Cordelia, scientist in charge of experimental synthetic cytology, took the trouble to lock the incubator and lock the laboratory door before leaving the State Biophysical Center. The thing in the main thermostatically controlled incubator was so vital that she felt constrained to deliver the progress report personally to the Senior Mistress of Applied Cytology in the Ministry of Biophysical Research.

Cordelia, a woman of seventy-two, had made full use of modern cosmetic techniques, and her metabolic control had been precisely judged for more than two decades. Consequently she had all the superficial appearance of an adolescent female, except for the maturity of her eyes and the overfull roundness of her breasts and abdomen, the result of three compulsory visits to State fertility centers where induced parthenogenesis had resulted in the birth, over four years, of eight identical baby girls.

But her mind was wrinkled and leathery, impregnated with specialized science and technology, and twisted in the accepted Lesbian fashion of contemporary society. The thing in the incubator was alien and incomprehensible, but it represented success. For centuries, perhaps millennia, women scientists had labored after the shadow, as alchemists of ancient history had sought the Philosopher's Stone, and now, finally, the shadow had taken shape. The thing in the incu-

154

bator represented the pinnacle of scientific achievement; and
it might also be the problem of all time.

She traveled by underground mobile roads to the select
government zone of the city, and ascended to the fourteenth
story of the Department of Science and Techonolgy. There
was some difficulty with the receptionist and the undersecre-
tary; the Senior Mistress of Applied Cytology was by no
means readily accessible. After a twenty minute delay she
was admitted to the secretary's office, and ten minutes later
finally reached the inner sanctum and found herself greeting
the Mistress herself.

The Mistress was a woman of indeterminate age, fleshy
without being fat, rigid without being bony. Her face was
flaccid, her eyes small but deep. Her flat breasts were lacquered purple as was the custom among higher government
officials. She wore a short black skirt and black sandals, con-
trasting with her hair which had been varnished snow white.

"Sit down, Cordelia," said the Mistress of Applied Cytology. "I must apologize for keeping you waiting, but pressure
of work is, well . . ." She smiled thinly. "Unexpected inter-
views are always difficult to arrange."

Cordelia nodded sympathetically. "I understand, Mistress.
But I have some very important news about test four-six-
five."

The Mistress opened a drawer in her desk and produced
a box file which she opened, withdrawing a number of
papers. She flicked through them rapidly, then selected one
particular typewritten sheet.

"Four-six-five," she murmured thoughtfully. "That's in the
chromosome linkage series."

"The Arctic man," Cordelia explained. "The one they found
in the ice three years ago."

"I remember."

"He was in a remarkably well-preserved state. We were
able to isolate many thousands of perfect cell nuclei—gam-

etes, of course—bearing twenty-three chromosomes. They were dead, but the chromosomes were transferable. It took a long time to perfect the technique: precision micro-cytology using scalpels invisible to the naked eye. We had to remove the chromosomes from a male gamete and transfer them to a living female ovum, matching them perfectly so that natural affinity would occur; so that the cell would live, and divide and grow, keeping its forty-seven chromosomes, growing and developing all the time . . ."

"I know; I know . . ."

"Well, the Arctic man was shared among eighteen cytological laboratories. I had an allocation of gametes along with the rest. Four days ago I performed my four hundred and sixty-fifth micro-cytological transfer."

"And . . . what happened?"

"I succeeded, Mistress. The cell is still alive. It has already divided and subdivided more than twenty times. Each new cell has forty-seven chromosomes. I've checked with the ultra-violet phase-contrast microscope. There's no mistake."

The Mistress of Applied Cytology pursed her lips and studied Cordelia as if she were a new virus strain. "In other words," she said, "you claim to have produced a living male embryo."

"Exactly."

"For the first time in five thousand years."

"Yes."

The Mistress stood up and wandered thoughtfully around the room, stroking her rectangular chin and frowning in mild perplexity, as if solving an obscure conundrum.

She said: "Which incubator are you using?"

"The Reissner thermostatic radiation chamber."

"I see. How long will it take for the embryo to develop beyond primary gestation?"

"With present parameters, temperature, and so on . . . about ten weeks . . ."

"With a positive physical determination of sex?"

"Yes."

The Mistress returned to her desk and made a note on a small note pad. "And you think it will live—this embryo?"

"I am certain of it. The cell division is vigorous and perfect in every way."

"Who else knows about this experiment?"

"My two assistants."

"What are their names?"

"Eupharia and Tosta. Do you want their registration numbers?"

The Mistress shook her head. "With an experiment of this type, particularly when successful, we have to make sure that there can be no possible leakage of information. You may take it, I think, that the Ministery will transfer Eupharia and Tosta almost immediately. They will also change the site of the experiment—the incubator and its associated equipment will be moved to a more secure location."

Cordelia blinked and opened her mouth as if about to speak, but said nothing. The Mistress of Applied Cytology smiled shallowly.

"This is not the first time we have had promising indications, of course. On many occasions cytologists have succeeded in creating a forty-seven chromosome embryo which divided and grew—for a short time. Naturally we are most anxious to avoid the spread of rumor and false information. Therefore we take stringent precautions."

"I understand," Cordelia murmured.

"We have a special laboratory reserved for what we define as alpha projects. What is more, we have a special staff of skilled and trained cytologists to take over such projects and develop them under carefully controlled conditions."

"You mean, I am to be relieved of my part in test four-six-five?"

"Not at all, Cordelia. You will work in liaison with our

alpha scientists. After all, you may be able to help them in many ways, initially."

"And then . . . ?"

"Well, if the project is successful, if the embryo survives and grows, then the alpha scientists will probably take over completely. You see, Cordelia, the development of a live male embryo is not purely an abstract scientific experiment. There are certain important social ramifications. There have been no live males in the world for some five thousand years, and an experiment like this, if it succeeds, must be considered from very many angles. It moves from the field of science into that of politics."

Cordelia eyed her superior thoughtfully, striving to read beyond the glassy inscrutable surface of the other woman's expressionless eyes. There was no sense of psychic contact; never had there been between people for as long as she could remember, except when the parthenogenetic adaptation syndrome produced emotional affinity that resolved itself in physical eroticism. A new and unwelcome idea invaded her brain. *We're robots, she and I,* Cordelia thought. *We're integers in some vast, impersonal social equation. We're not even individuals because we do not have the right of individual action any more. We are part of the mechanism, cells in the superior planetary body of integrated womankind, and our brain is an electronic brain and our conduct is controlled and predicted by a myriad electronic computing units.*

The feeling came and went, phantomlike. The Mistress condensed into solid humanity again and her hard fleshy face became earthy and workaday. In a hundred years it would be a sallow, gleaming skull.

"Return to your laboratory," said the Mistress. "Meanwhile I shall confer with the Ministry. In the course of a few hours I shall communicate with you and give you detailed instructions."

"And my assistants—what shall I tell them?"

The Mistress moved her lips into the shape of a grin. "By the time you reach your laboratory they will already have gone. You will never see them again."

The new laboratory was a subsection of the secret research center of the Ministry's Department of Applied Cytology. It was located more than a hundred feet below the ground, directly beneath the tall skyscraper that housed the immense staff of the Ministry of Biophysical Research. Cordelia had never even suspected the existence of the place, which was not surprising in view of the fantastic security precautions. She found that she was obliged to live underground, in a small apartment adjacent to the laboratory. Ten other research cytologists lived underground too. For three months she worked and slept beyond sight of sky or sunlight, breathing chemically conditioned air, living in perpetual artificial light, working at the gleaming chrome and plastic benches or the shining incubators, sleeping naked under the ultraviolet strip lamps that kept her body bronzed and healthy. She worked under orders, for she was no longer a responsible scientist in her own right; she was part of a team, and the other cytologists were women who had been specially selected for work of high security value. Security, it seemed, mattered more than scientific ability.

Test four-six-five was not the only experiment in progress. She was astonished to find that there were seventeen male embryos in the thermostatically controlled incubators of the laboratory: the one she had originated, and sixteen others. And one by one they died. It was one thing to create a male embryo, but quite another to secure its survival.

Her colleagues, she soon knew, were experienced in synthetic embryology. They knew all the answers, while she was still in the phase of asking questions. The embryos died, and they knew exactly why they had died, but they could do nothing about it. But embryo four-six-five, incredibly, did

not die. It was a matter of indefinables, of some subtlety in
the exact mechanism of surgical micro-cytology, of some precise factor in the artificial synthesis of a male gamete. It was
some unpredictable phenomenon in advanced biochemistry,
in discrete cell physiology. It was a phenomenon that might
not be reproduced again for a decade, or a hundred years,
or ever again. All in all, a miracle, but a miracle of patiently
applied science over a long period.

The embryo grew and grew, and began to differentiate.
Limbs began to appear, and a head and a beating heart. The
artificial placenta supplied oxygenated blood to the tiny living creature, and the saline solution in which it was immersed
was maintained precisely at a temperature of ninety-eight
point four degrees Fahrenheit.

Gestation was rapid, accelerated by carefully conceived
electronic control, by automation applied to human embryology. Cordelia's estimate of ten weeks proved to be a little
on the pessimistic side. At the end of eight weeks the embryo was already a male child weighing four pounds and
more, still attached to the artificial placenta, but moving its
limbs with aggressive energy. It became apparent that the
child would, within the fortnight, be ready for independent
existence, ready for severing from the placenta and removal
from the saline solution, ready to learn to breath and cry and
suckle on electronically fed teats. Or, as Cordelia recognized
with a faint feeling of revulsion which had its origin in compulsory fertility and parthenogenesis, ready for birth.

Her own interest in the male child grew steadily from day
to day. This was something quite different from the normal
routine procedure of birth. Females were being produced
on what might almost be regarded as an assembly line basis
every hour of the day, but here was a male, growing and
developing under experimental laboratory conditions. A creature unique in time and space, unique, at any rate, for five
millennia.

Sometimes she fell to speculating about the future of the child, her child, in the incubator. What role could a male fulfill in a monosexual society that had adapted itself to its own peculiar mode of existence and survival for longer than anyone could remember? Was there any point or purpose in allowing the child to survive? And supposing there were more male children, supposing the child, on attaining maturity, would be able to reproduce its own sex in defiance of the natural inhibition that had operated for so many centuries: What then? Could society turn the clock back and resume heterosexual living? Could women tolerate reversion to the primitive in matters of human propagation? Induced parthenogenesis was neater, cleaner and so precise. Devoid of emotional contamination, and pure in that it was a function on the level of abstract duty, it was impregnation by the unseen and the unfelt. Radiation was surely the ultimate in reproductive technique, and no modern woman could contemplate without horror any kind of crude physical fertilization by a creature that had been obsolete for thousands of years. It was unimaginable.

And yet there was something appealing about the child in the incubator, something that occasionally caught the heart, like an injection of adrenalin, and produced an indescribable writhing of the fundamental emotions. And Cordelia was conscious of a very special feeling of proprietorship, for it was she who had performed the original micro-cytological operation that had injected the breath of life into the pink and wrinkled midget inside the glass case. The child was hers, as surely as if she personally had given birth to it in a State fertility center.

As the child grew and reached the stage of imminent independence, she experienced something akin to pride, and presently, to love.

On the day they removed the male child from the incuba-

tor and slapped it into a lusty bawling, the Senior Mistress of
Applied Cytology visited the underground laboratory. Her
square jaw was firm and unsympathetic, and her eyes cold.
Cordelia sensed, in subdued alarm, a certain critical quality
in her attitude.

The Mistress inspected the child, but betrayed no reaction.

"Weight?" she enquired.

"Eight pounds, four ounces," Cordelia announced proudly,
as if she personally had given birth to the baby.

The Mistress's eyes traveled the length of the tiny male in
the enclosed plastic crib.

"There's no denying the maleness."

Cordelia said nothing; there was an acrid quality in her
superior's voice that she did not like. Two or three of the
other scientists had gathered round to hear the Mistress's
comments. They were impassive in their attitude: the baby
might have been a stained specimen on a microscope slide
for all the human interest that was apparent in their eyes.
Cordelia began to feel angry, and, more surprisingly, pro-
tective towards the infant under scrutiny.

"During the past weeks," said the Mistress, "test four-six-
five has been discussed at high level throughout the world.
A *very* high level, if I may say so. Needless to say our executive scientists and politicians have acted in close liaison with
the world electronic brain network, so you will appreciate
that any decision they have reached is the result of long and
careful consideration."

Cordelia found herself resenting the label that had been
attached to her baby—test four-six-five—and, fearing the somber implication of the word "decision," she said nothing; but
waited for the Mistress to continue.

"You will understand that for a long, long time the prin-
cipal object of scientific research in our world of today has
been"—she waved a hand idly towards the crib—"this. What

you see before you, alive and unbelievably active, is the end product of millions of experiments over hundreds of years—*secret* experiments. The outside world knows nothing of what we have attempted to do. Womankind as a whole has adapted herself to life as we know it, and in the course of time a very stable and efficient form of society has been developed. We live, and live very well indeed, without a male sex; so much so that it is questionable whether society would be any the better off if a reversion to bisexual conditions were to occur."

A murmur of agreement rippled round her audience. The Mistress was merely echoing opinions that had been inbred since birth in all of them.

"Nevertheless, it has always been the policy of the government to control every factor that might influence the structure of our society, and it has always been realized that a species without a male sex might, in some way, be lacking in some fundamental psychological component that . . . well, to put it simply, would maintain overall human sanity."

"Nonsense," said one of the cytologists, smiling. "As a race we are saner than ever before in history."

"Why," said another, echoing the smug good humor of her colleague, "we all know that the age of insanity was the age of men. Every child is taught that in the State school."

The Mistress smiled grimly. "Governmental policy is rather different from what is taught in State schools. Racial sanity is more than a question of racial behavior. It involves deep psychology on a mass basis, a racial neurosis, if you like. There are very good reasons for believing that the stable form of society in which we live is essentially neurotic." She scanned her audience like a radar antenna. "A neurosis can be extremely stable, particularly when it is based on a long established perversion. That is the condition of our society today."

Murmurs of doubtful assent and disguised bewilderment.

"All this is not merely a personal opinion. It is fact. Behind it is the authority of the sociological data bank of the world brain. Human society is cast in the form of a perversion neurosis. But it has achieved equilibrium. The perversion is exactly balanced by a seat of artificial ethics: law, behavior, relationships, moralities designed to channel the perversion into useful and productive streams of human energy. And designed to make the women of the world happy."

"What is all this leading up to, Mistress?" asked Cordelia. The other women seemed to withdraw a little at her temerity. But the Mistress simply made a pleasant face, as if she had been expecting the question and regarded it as an enthusiastic invitation to continue.

"I will come to that presently," said the Mistress in a not-to-be-hurried tone of voice. "First I want to stress the fundamentals of the problem which has confronted us. It is both simple and complex. We have to deal with a stable perversion-neurosis in which the operation conditions are a strict, impersonal totalitarianism of government, coupled, strangely enough, with an almost universal happiness. You see, the unhappy ones, those who have not adapted themselves readily to the parthenogenetic syndrome, are steadily weeded out. Our mortic revenue laws see to that, and what is more, they see to it in a manner apparently unconnected with parthenogenesis. The mortic laws are a subtle form of eugenic breeding, and in the course of time all women will conform to the pattern of the syndrome and must therefore be perfectly happy and contented."

There was a general atmosphere of uneasiness among the audience. Other cytologists had joined the group, and they stood listening restlessly, avoiding the direct gaze of the Mistress's eyes, listening closely, but in a manner which suggested that they should not be listening to all.

The Mistress's voice became more somber in tone. "I am

telling you things which some of you, perhaps most of you, have only vaguely suspected. As trusted government servants you already know more than the rest of womankind. You know the true secret of induced parthenogenesis, and you probably realize why we propagate the belief that parthenogenesis is largely of natural origin. It is all part of the syndrome, part of the mechanism which ensures a stable society. But I have hinted at a greater control, a firmer grasp on human affairs. Don't let it surprise you. Human affairs are no longer human; they are predicted and conducted by efficient electronic brains. The world brain network is always right. It is immensely wise and it never makes a mistake."

Cordelia ventured to speak again. It was the only *way* of relieving the anxiety that was building up in her mind. "All this is most interesting, Mistress, but what has it to do with test four-six-five." She felt ashamed of herself for referring to her baby by the official label, but the words were uttered and could not be recalled. She glanced towards the crib. The child was awake, and kicking with small wrinkled legs, and possibly crying, but no sound could penetrate the sealed plastic walls of the enclosure. At all events test four-six-five was a reality, and there was little anyone could do about it, even an electronic brain.

"Test four-six-five must be destroyed," said the Mistress crisply.

A multiple gasp quivered momentarily in the air as the audience reacted to the edict. Cordelia found herself suddenly chilled and shaking, but the feeling passed quickly, and anger took its place.

"Did you say destroyed?" she enquired icily.

The Mistress's eyes noted with a slight flicker the defiant note in Cordelia's voice. She smiled and her lips curved into benevolent charm.

"That is the final decision of the world brain. Believe me,

it was made only after many weeks of the most careful computation and research into sociological science."

Cordelia glanced hastily around the frozen circle of her colleagues and was encouraged by the dismay reflected in their expressions. She pointed to the baby. "This is no longer a test embryo, Mistress; it is a live independent human being. To destroy it would be murder."

"Not in law," said the Mistress smoothly. "The Department of Applied Cytology realized a long time ago that special provision would have to be made for experimental embryos undergoing development tests in laboratories. At one time all such living embryos were regraded as individuals—premature humans, in a sense—but obviously such an attitude could only hinder the progress of scientific research; therefore, the law was modified. All experimental embryos of laboratory origin are regarded as expendable test material unless application is made to the Department of Mortic Revnue for recognition of any particular test embryo as a human individual in law."

"Then let us make the application now."

"There would be no point. Mortic policy is determined by world brain computations, and the brain has already given its verdict. The Department of Mortic Revenue could not now give recognition to test four-six-five."

A profound silence blanketed the group. Only the faint remote ticking of the thermostats in the incubators disturbed the noiselessness, as if underlining the significance of the Mistress's words. Incubators, cytological experiments, embryos, expendable material—the jargon of a cold, dispassionate science. For a few moments everyone, it seemed, except the Mistress, was looking at the baby.

"Beware of sentiment," said the Mistress, her voice controlled and calm. "What you see in the crib in the result of a successful experiment in micro-cytology, the end product of cell division and differentiation. It is a test subject, a specimen. There is no question of human status. Other embryos have had to be destroyed, and there is no difference of principle in this case."

The baby was unconcernedly sucking its thumb, not caring about status or principles. Cordelia noted the clear blue eyes moving restlessly as if trying to make sense out of the shapes and lights and human figures beyond the plastic walls of the crib. They were intelligent eyes, human eyes.

Cordelia said: "May we know why the world brain thought it desirable to destroy this—this child?"

"It is not a child; it is a test specimen," said the Mistress sharply. "I have already warned you about the dangers of sentiment. Judgment must always be free from emotional contamination."

"And from mercy?"

"To talk of mercy in connection with a test specimen is meaningless. However, let me explain how the verdict was obtained. Perhaps it will help to resolve your doubts and demonstrate the inevitable rightness of the brain's decision. The problem was basically one of introducing an unknown variable factor into a balanced social equation. We had to examine the many millions of permutations and combinations of possible social change that could result from the introduction of one live male into society as it now exists. We took into account the question of male reproduction, and even assumed for the purposes of computation that within a certain number of generations the male sex, if it were perpetuated, might equal the female in numbers, as was once the case. We found that a stable heterosexual society might be possible in five thousand years. But during the intervening period there would be chaos. Society as we know it would disintegrate."

"But why?"

The Mistress sighed patiently. "Because of the syndrome, the perversion-neurosis. It was caused by the elimination of man. If you confront a pervert-neurotic with the cause of all the trouble and try to enforce a reversion to normal behavior, the result will almost certainly be hysteria. And hysteria on a mass basis is a terrible thing. It means an end to rational thought and conduct, a disruption of normal activity. Worse still, it means a lack of control, racial insanity, and racial suicide."

"You mean," said Cordelia ominously, "that once women realized that men were returning into their lives, they would rebel against this regimentation, this carefully planned Lesbian society. They would laugh at the syndrome, as you call it, and tear your beautifully organized social structure to pieces in sheer mutiny."

"You know that's not true," the Mistress said quietly. "It is not a question of rebellion or mutiny, for there is nothing to rebel against. I repeat: Society is stable. The subversive element is negligible, and we keep it under control by deep hypnotic techniques. The problem is purely one of hysteria. Human behavior would become unpredictable, and that is a bad thing. There would be widespread unhappiness, and that is even worse. There might be outbreaks of violence, suicide, and non-co-operation in parthenogenetic matters. I'm sure you would not like to see this happen."

"If the world knew that a male child had been born there would be a sudden change in female psychology."

"That is exactly what I said—hysteria."

"You're afraid that the government would be undermined, would lose its power to govern. You're afraid that someone might decide to wreck the world brain in the cause of freedom and independence. Well, let them wreck it! Is stability so important after all, or even happiness? Are human beings the better for being predictable, even though they are pervert-neurotics? Perhaps five thousand years of hysteria and chaos might be worth-while if it results in a new kind of society with both males and females. Even the beasts of the field have *that* privilege!"

Cordelia became silent, alarmed and astonished at the trend of her speech. The words had spilled themselves from her brain without conscious thought, and they did not even represent her true attitude. She was a loyal member of the State, a trusted government scientist, and never in her life had she voiced or even entertained ideas of such a treasonable nature, nor did she even believe what she had just said. The words had tumbled from some dark region beyond consciousness, uncontrollably, as if generated by some new irrational twist in her brain. *Hysteria*, she thought, suddenly afraid. *The male child had started it. Test four-six-five: the pink specimen in the plastic case. The Mistress had been right, and the syndrome was real. Already hysteria was insidiously affecting her judgment, injecting unreason into her thoughts, introducing an element of unpredictability into her reactions.*

She saw her diagnosis confirmed in the hard set of the Mistress's eyes and in the restrained alarm of her colleagues. She had confirmed, by her words, everything that the Mistress had said, and it was too late now to retract or apologize. The inevitable would happen: she would be taken away to a psychoneural center and subjected to deep hypnosis to rid her mind of the distortion that had revealed itself so clearly. In time she would be transferred to a new post in a new city. And test four-six-five would be destroyed anyway.

She had risked her future for nothing.

"I think," said the Mistress, "that you had better come with me, Cordelia. Meanwhile, destroy test four-six-five!"

XVI

AFTER Cordelia and the Mistress had gone, the cytologists in the laboratory talked among themselves. The conversation bore multiple symptoms of shock, alarm, embarrassment and self-righteousness. Only Koralin had nothing to say; she was a junior scientist, not yet thirty, of an introspective nature. She listened closely without change of expression, but did not contribute to the general discussion.

"Whoever would have imagined . . . Cordelia, of all people."

"You can never tell. The quiet, conscientious ones are often the most unreliable."

"But to behave in that way . . ."

"And just after the Mistress had been talking about hysteria . . ."

"It illustrates the danger of specialization. Cordelia had worked for a long time on test four-six-five. She must have developed some emotional attachment . . ."

"It's fatal. A scientist must always be objective."

"I admit it is difficult to regard test four-six-five purely as a specimen, but after all, facts are facts."

"If we all started getting sentimental about every embryo in the incubators, where would we be?"

"What do you suppose will happen to her?"

"Nothing much . . . a little psychoneural treatment. The State is very lenient."

"But to talk about destroying the world brain . . ."

"Hysteria, my dear. She didn't really know what she was saying. As if anyone could ever interfere with the brain . . ."

"Do you suppose there are other women like her?"

"One or two. There is always an element of insanity in any kind of society."

"I can't help feeling that the brain is right. After all, what woman would really want to see men return to society?"

"We might as well humanize apes and gorillas."

"How horrible! It must have been terrible, five thousand years ago, I mean . . . before they discovered induced parthenogenesis."

"I don't think anyone would want to go back to such times. They say men used to run the world, and women were virtually slaves. Men used to use them as they wished, whenever they wished; not only when they wanted children, but all the time. Sometimes every week, sometimes every day."

"No . . . ! Even the animals . . ."

"And there were wars, conflicts during which nations used to destroy each other with atomic weapons. And churches, where men would go once a week to be forgiven of their sins."

"We have a great deal to be thankful for. The Mistress was right. At least we are happy."

"We are more than happy. We are fortunate beyond imagination. We have achieved a Utopia that could never have been attained if men had survived."

"True. The world would have been destroyed thousands of years ago—other worlds too. Men always thought in terms of exploration and destruction: first our own Earth, then the planets Mars, Venus, and the others. They were moving in that direction. By now the entire solar system would have been destroyed in atomic fire."

"Poor Cordelia. How misguided she is."

"There's no need to feel sorry for her. The State will look after her and remove the taint from her mind and give her happiness."

"I suppose so. She doesn't really deserve it. To say such things to the Senior Mistress of Applied Cytology!"

"And all over an experimental embryo. It hardly seems worth it."

"Who is going to destroy test four-six-five?"

Koralin said: "I will."

The women regarded her curiously.

"Please," Koralin went on. "Let me destroy the specimen. I feel so strongly about it. I should like to destroy it; I feel I should be serving the Mistress in a direct way."

"How do you propose to do it?" asked the senior cytologist, an elderly woman of silver hair and narrow face.

"Parametrically," Koralin said. "Even the destruction of a useless embryo can be useful. I should like to make a series of tests to examine oxygen consumption, reducing the level minute by minute to the point of death."

"Excellent. I see you have the correct scientific attitude, Koralin."

"It occurred to me that even at this stage we might learn something about male physiology. And that knowledge might help medical science in some way."

"Good, but we must not delay the killing by too long. The Mistress's instructions were quite precise, and they made no provision for experiment."

"One hour," said Koralin. "That's all I ask. It will give me an opportunity to make blood tests and check on brain wave-forms as the oxygen content of the blood is reduced to zero."

"Very well," said the senior cytologist. "You may destroy test four-six-five. Let me know if you obtain any data of interest."

"I will," Koralin promised.

Koralin transferred the baby to a sealed oxygen chamber and regulated the flow of gas to normal intake. Several of her colleagues watched her for a few minutes, but presently they grew bored, and wandered off to pursue their own tasks. Koralin found herself alone with the male child.

There was no hurry. What she was about to do required the utmost calmness and self-possession, and it was essential that she should not be observed. She busied herself for a few minutes with instruments, occasionally moving over to the crib and examining the child, as if making a preliminary physical survey. Presently she crossed to a screened recess containing vials and bottles of drugs and chemicals, and lei-surely, though carefully, filled a hypodermic syringe from a tiny rubber-capped green vial. She injected the contents of the syringe into the baby. It cried for an instant in outraged

anger, then suddenly became quiescent and, after a few
moments, stiffened like a waxen doll.

Satisfied, she surveyed the laboratory. The other women
appeared to be engrossed in their own work. Some were peering into microscopes; others were engaged at the incubator
rack, carrying on the routine of cytology and embryology
as if the research program were unchanging and eternal.
They had not yet realized that it had come to a stop, that
there would be no further experiments to manufacture a
living male cell. Their minds were so drilled that they would
continue in the pattern of their work until the official order
arrived. Cease work. We are no longer interested in creating
a male. Why? Because we succeeded and found that society
would be better off without it. Further research along these
lines has no object, and no possible justification.

But there was no longer any time for introspective reflection. The moment for action had come. Quickly she loosened
her white smock so that it hung shapelessly around her, then
opened the oxygen chamber and lifted the baby out, slipping
it beneath the smock and holding it awkwardly to conceal
the bulge. As an additional precaution she crossed to the
Records Annex and picked up a sheaf of papers which she
held in front of her, then feeling that her burden was reasonably well disguised, walked swiftly from the laboratory to
the domestic quarters. In her own room she laid the baby
gently upon her bed.

Staring thoughtfully down at it, she was struck suddenly
by the foolhardiness of what she had done. Without pre-
meditation, and with only a hurried minimum of planning
she had embarked on the first dangerous step of what she
could only envisage as the absolutely impossible. Anxiety
hardened the faint lines round her brown eyes; her long triangular face, normally ascetic and acrid, reflected a shadow
of apprehension. Awareness of insecurity modulated the thin
curve of her lips.

She stroked her cropped black hair with nervous fingers, oblivious to the fragments of old varnish that broke away at the contact. Her mind was making a tentative reconnaissance of the immediate future.

One thing was certain: She could not afford to remain in the building a moment longer than necessary. Once the alarm had been raised security police would be mobilized in force. Every second of delay meant increasing jeopardy. No time to stop and think; it was imperative to keep on the move. One could always think while moving.

She hunted in a cupboard for a sheet of paper and a plastic shopping bag. Carefully she lifted the inert child and slipped the paper beneath it, then proceeded to make a compact parcel, which she packed carefully into the bottom of the plastic bag. On top of the paper bundle she placed a folded crimson cloak.

Then, satisfied that the carrier was to all appearances innocent, she picked it up and left the room, making her way with as much nonchalance as she could muster to the swift silent elevator that led to ground level and the open city.

There was no trouble with the security guards at the main exit. They knew her as a member of the scientific staff and the shopping bag was too ordinary to arouse suspicion. She walked for two blocks, then took a velocab, and traveled to Kinkross station, a central terminal for the high-speed monorail trains which covered the country on atomic jet units.

She had to get out of Lon as quick as possible, and she knew where she was going. Some years ago she had had a friend called Deurina, a beautiful albino with a parthenogenetic twin sister named Aquilegia, and there had been another woman known as Aubretia who had been a security risk at one time. It was a point of contact worth pursuing. There seemed to be no alternative for the moment.

She bought a ticket to the city of Birm.

For Aubretia it had been a tiring day. After nearly three years of working in the local Department of Statistics, collating and filing government records, she was beginning to find the routine of the civil service tedious. To add to her restlessness, she was uneasily aware of a certain indefinable mental aberration: the occasional breakthrough of illusory half-memories of some other kind of life that could not be precisely pinpointed. It was as if, intermittently, she were some other person, in a curious elusive dream, and yet there seemed to be no rational explanation for this strange delusion.

Coinciding with the development of this disquieting twist in her mind came a growing coldness towards her friend, Valinia, the olive-skinned, erotic girl in the apartment below. Valinia was becoming, in some inexplicable way, alien. She was too expert in every way, in her knowledge of government policy and social structure, in her profound understanding of erotic science, and in her grasp of applied psychology. Lately, Aubretia found herself beginning to wonder just how much of the other girl's friendship was genuine and sincere, and how much was motivated by some unguessable purpose.

At present Valinia was away on one of her regular three day trips out of town. Aubretia was not sure where, visiting whom, or for what reason? Reporting, perhaps, to the headquarters of the Department of Internal Security? That was a thought which, though it had once seemed fantastic and ludicrous, was no longer completely unacceptable. On the other hand, why security? There was nothing in either her own or Valinia's past to arouse the interest of the security people, nothing she could recall. On the other hand, there were those recurring fragments of illusory half-memory . . .

When the doorbell chimed she sensed a certain relief. Visitors were a distraction, and they helped to restore the reality of here and now, and dispel the phantom impression that kept intruding upon the privacy of her mind.

She opened the door and found herself face to face with a gaunt-featured yet not unattractive young woman with sensitive and troubled eyes. In her right hand she was carrying a plastic shopping bag, clutching the handle tightly as if afraid it might be unexpectedly snatched from her grasp.

Aubretia smiled politely: some quality behind the stranger's eyes disarmed her. There was a pleasant feeling of psychic resonance, of two minds in tune.

"Are you the woman they call Aubretia?" asked the stranger.

Aubretia nodded.

"May I come in? It is very important."

Aubretia led the way into the mellow light of the apartment. She switched off the video screen and gestured towards a chair. The dark haired girl set the shopping bag carefully on the table, then sat down, remaining poised on the edge of the chair as if unable to relax.

"Who are you?" Aubretia enquired.

"My name is Koralin. I am a cytologist in the Department of Biophysical Research . . . or, rather, I *was*. I had a friend called Deurina, an albino."

Aubretia shook her head slowly, as if the information were meaningless to her.

"She had an identical twin, also an albino. Her name was Aquilegia."

Aubretia's expression became suddenly transfixed and her eyes were, for an instant, remote and far away, but the mood passed almost as quickly as it had begun. The ghost of an albino woman had been hovering in the darker fringes of her mind for a long time now, and at the mention of the name Aquilegia the ghost had become brighter, more clearly etched. Deurina also clicked into place as a very real memory. There *had* been an albino woman, three years ago, and she *had* claimed to be the sister of someone called Aquilegia, though she had never given her own name. What had happened to her, Aubretia wondered? Suddenly the past returned in disconcerting detail: the subversive talk, the somber revelation of secret laboratories, and something that had to do with a man, and later, in the deep night, the quiet phone call to the police. She had never seen Deurina again.

"You remember; you must remember," urged Koralin.

Aubretia passed a hand wearily across her brow. "Vaguely, one or two things. Why did you come here?"

"Because Deurina was my friend, just as her sister Aquilegia was yours. That must give us something in common."

"All right, Koralin, supposing it does, what do you want of me?"

"First a promise that whatever I say will be a secret between us. I must have absolute trust in you."

"I owe you that trust. I betrayed Deurina. At the time I thought it was the right thing to do. Since then . . . well, things have been happening to my mind. Now I'm no longer sure of anything."

Koralin stood up, placing one hand protectively on the plastic bag, and eyed Aubretia uncertainly. "I didn't know, about Deurina, I mean. I knew she came here after she left the laboratory. She was in trouble with security, and when she disappeared I thought it was just that security had finally caught up with her . . ."

"Security did—at my invitation. I can't explain it. I seem to remember that Deurina said they'd been to work on my mind. I never understood what she meant, and I'm not sure that I do even now . . ."

"You were once the Press Policy Officer for the Department of the Written Word, weren't you, Aubretia?"

"I can't remember."

"But you *were*. Until you made a mistake. Aquilegia had been talking to you, explaining some of the secrets of our society as it exists, not as we are taught to believe it exists. You made a mistake by trying to release the information

over the public press and broadcast services. Your message
never got any further than the memory banks in the news
offices, where it was promptly cancelled. They took you away
and gave you the treatment, a deep hypnotic reorientation of
your mind. They arrested Aquilegia, and they closed in on
Deurina. She slipped away, for a few days, and, well, you
know the rest . . ."

Aubretia's eyes were thoughtful and introspective. "I don't
remember, Koralin; honestly I don't. Only the things that
happened after I came to Birm mean anything at all. The
rest is just . . . fragments of some kind of weird dream."

"It will come back to you, not all at once, but slowly. I'll
try to help you, Aubretia."

"But why? I'm a secure citizen. Why should I become
involved in subversive business?"

"Afraid of your mortic record?"

"My record is good so far as I know."

Koralin removed the crimson cloak from the plastic carrier, then carefully lifted out the paper wrapped bundle and
placed it on the table.

"I came to you for help," she said. "Not many of us can
see through the sham of our way of living, and even fewer
know the full truth. Most of the subversive types are already
under security surveillance, though they may not realize it."

Aubretia nodded in silence, thinking of Valinia.

"In the ordinary way," Koralin said, placing one hand on
the bundle, "we should never have met, not in a thousand
years. I would have spent my life in the Department of Biophysical Research, and you would have remained in the
Department of Statistics. But today something important
happened, something that might affect the future of the entire world."

Aubretia's eyes became questioning.

"Today," Koralin went on, "a decision was made at a high
level. It was a decision with which I disagreed. One of my

colleagues also disagreed, but she was foolish enough to say
so. Right now she is probably undergoing hypnotic reorientation."

"What was the decision?"

Koralin began unwrapping the bundle. Her hands moved
slowly, methodically. With a touch of melodrama she kept
the contents covered by the paper until she was ready to per-
form the unveiling ceremony. Then she said: "The world
brain decided, after many weeks of careful consideration,
that *this should be destroyed . .*"

She unveiled the baby in a crackling flourish of paper.

XVII

THE Controller of Internal Security switched off the videophone and pressed a green button on the intercom panel.

"Get me the Senior Mistress of Applied Cytology in Zone
Four."

"Yes, ma'am."

Fifteen seconds of silence, then a metallic voice through
the intercom grille.

"Applied Cytology. Senior Mistress speaking."

The Controller faded up the video screen. A flaccid,
square-jawed face stared at her from beyond the rectangular
panel of glass.

"Code six," said the Controller curtly.

The image on the screen glanced downwards. Unseen fingers moved an unseen switch. Scrambler circuits clicked
into operation to render the conversation indecipherable at
all intermediate points between the two terminals.

"I have received an alarming report," said the Controller.
"It concerns you."

"Indeed?"

"And test four-six-five."

The Mistress smiled a little. "Test four-six-five has been destroyed."

"Are you certain?"

"I gave the order myself."

"And you witnessed the destruction and checked the death of the embryo, pathologically?"

"Not personally. It was unnecessary. The staff of the cytological laboratory can be trusted to obey orders."

"All of them?"

The Mistress's face became a little smug. "With one exception, a woman called Cordelia who proved to have certain reversionist ideas. I have arranged for a course of hypno-orientation. She will not return to the laboratory."

"Supposing I were to tell you that test four-six-five was not destroyed."

Another smile. A little shallower. "That would be highly improbable."

The Controller said nothing, just watched the screen with inscrutable eyes. The smile of the image faded slowly.

"The specimen must have been destroyed within a few minutes of my leaving the laboratory. I am confident it was done, efficiently. Naturally, I could not wait; there was the woman named Cordelia to escort to a place of supervision."

"I think," said the Controller gently, "that you had better come here. There are things we must talk about."

The image of the Mistress froze. Fear darkened her eyes for an instant.

"You mean . . . ?"

"I mean, Mistress, that test four-six-five is still alive. Not only that, but the specimen has been removed from the laboratory. I'm afraid you might be in serious trouble."

"I'll be right over," said the Mistress faintly.

After the image had faded from the screen, the Controller thumbed the intercom again.

"I want to send a broadcast message to all security units

and headquarters throughout the world. Code six. Priority Emergency. Tactics urgent military. Subject act of utmost subversion. Two hours ago the living body of a male child produced from an experimental embryo was stolen from a cytological laboratory in Lon, Zone Four, by a woman named Koralin. This woman must be apprehended without fail, using all emergency security tactics. The child, which has not received mortic classification as human, must be instantly destroyed and incinerated. This order is based on the authority of the world brain network."

She paused and referred to a file of papers.

"In a moment I shall give you a detailed description of the woman Koralin, and an indication of her probable movements, following which an immediate total security check is to be placed on all airports, seaports, road and rail transport stations, and provisioning centers. All vehicles entering and leaving all towns and cities are to be stopped and searched. All pedestrians carrying parcels or bundles or carriers of any kind are to be halted and searched. This is an emergency operation."

A pause, then: "Here is a detailed description of the woman Koralin . . ."

"It is a male child," said Koralin, unable to conceal a nuance of pride in her voice. "Test four-six-five is the official designation. The micro-cytology operation was performed by a woman named Cordelia. When the embryo started to grow, we took over."

Aubretia, incredulous and vaguely horrified, was inspecting the pale still body of the baby from a distance, her fingers touching her cheek in abject uncertainty.

"But . . . but it's *dead!*"

"No. Merely unconscious. I injected paracain. The child will sleep for about thirty hours."

"Then what . . . ?"

"The Senior Mistress of Applied Cytology this morning
gave the order for the destruction of this child. You realize
what that would have meant?"

"No . . ."

"It would have meant the end of all hope for the per-
verted and neurotic society in which we live. It would have
been the final act of despotism, establishing for all time the
robot state: female automatons working to the orders of
electronic computors. This baby,"—Koralin touch the infant
gently—"could be the savior of womankind."

"Savior . . ?"

"I realize I'm talking about things you may not fully understand, but believe me, Aubretia, what I am saying to
you is the truth. The last man died some five thousand years
ago. Women would have died too, if scientists had not
learned how to perpetuate the human species by artificial
means. But a monosexual society must of necessity be a per-
verted society—abnormal. It conforms to distorted patterns
of behavior, and for that reason is all the more susceptible
to regimentation. You have heard of the parthenogenetic
adaptation syndrome. It is a concise definition of our way
of life. It sounds like a disease, and that's exactly what it is.
We are diseased, all of us, and we shall go on being diseased,
generation after generation, until the end of time. Unless
. . ."

"Unless," Aubretia repeated hollowly, not comprehend-
ing, but sensing the ominous implications of the other woman's argument.

"Unless we turn the clock back five thousand years. Unless
we reintroduce a male sex and revert to a normal way of
living."

"But, would it be normal?"

Koralin smiled grimly. "Study ancient history. Consider
nature as a whole. Think of life and living. Then look
around you at the world we know: laboratories, experiments

in human embryology, fertility centers, induced parthenogenesis, the syndrome, cultivated Lesbianism. Don't you
feel that something is missing?"

"No . . . but sometimes, yes. I have a feeling, but I can't
define it."

"Would you want the world to go on in this way for the
next ten thousand years?"

Aubretia spread her hands uncertainly. "I don't think I
shall have any feelings about it a hundred years from now."

"That is the voice of deep hypnosis, Aubretia. There was a
time when you were concerned about the state of the world
today, sufficiently concerned to risk your future, even your
life, by committing an act of major subversion."

"I don't remember."

"But you will. I'll help you to remember."

Aubretia walked slowly across the room to the window
and looked out into the night with its twinkling firmament
of colored neons. "All I know is you have brought here a
male child which should have been destroyed. Why, Koralin? Tell me why?"

"Because a point in time had been reached when human
affairs could change, once only, and for the last time. I was
assigned to destroy the child Had I done so the future
would have become static, for there will never be another
male child. This is the first, and the last. I injected paracain
and stole the child, and came straight here."

"But you can't get away with it, Koralin. Once they find
out there is no corner of the world where you will be safe.
They will seek you out, and they will take the child and
destroy it anyway, and perhaps you too. What will you have
gained?"

"About seven thousand years ago," Koralin said quietly,
after a pause, "there was another parthenogenetic male, a
miracle child that was referred to as the savior of mankind.
The State set out systematically to destroy it; to destroy

all new born males. It was the same kind of security, ruthlessly applied, by an authority which feared the child's power
to undermine authority. But they failed. The child survived . . ."

"Well . . . ?"

"History can repeat itself. Here we have another parthenogenetic male with the power to change the nature of society.
to undermine the authority of the State, to bring about a new
way of life and give new hope. For thousands of years the
world has awaited a second Messiah. And now he has arrived,
Aubretia, and authority will attempt to destroy him before
he destroys it."

"I don't know what you're talking about, Koralin; I don't
even know what the word Messiah means. But you're right
about authority. Security police will be on patrol now, everywhere. They'll be interrogating thousands, blocking all roads,
checking on provisioning centers, searching apartments.
Whatever may have happened seven thousand years ago, it
can't happen now. The child is as good as dead."

Koralin shook her head firmly. "Never. He is only a tiny
creature, easy to hide and easy to nourish. I can't do it alone,
Aubretia, but a group of us· you and me, then others we
could trust. Together we could conceal him and keep him
alive to grow and mature."

"How long would that take?"

"Eighteen, twenty years. Perhaps much less."

Aubretia sighed wearily. "You know it's impossible Twenty
is an eternity, and in a block of apartments like this . . .
There is a woman who lives below me: I feel sure she is a
security agent."

"We should have to escape. Move out of the city, perhaps
to some other part of the world. In a small community, beyond the reach of security . . ."

"There is no such place."

"But there is, Aubretia; there must be. Central Africa, or Antarctica . . ."

"How could you raise a child under such conditions?"

Koralin's lips were pressed into a stubborn line. "By constant care and attention. A dozen of us would do it, and the movement would spread and grow strong. As the child matured there would be thousands of us, and when he was old enough to effect fertilization, then there would be more male children, and they too would grow and mature . . ."

"You're dreaming, Koralin. You could never take the child more than half a dozen paces outside this building, and you know it."

"There are ways and means. I should have to stay here for a few days. There would be time to think and make plans, perhaps time to contact other women I know who would be sympathetic."

Aubretia crossed to the other woman and regarded her solemnly "You're a courageous woman, Koralin, but what you say is impossible. You are thinking in terms of starting some kind of colony in opposition to the world, and in defiance of the world brain." A coldly considered pause. "It couldn't work."

"It could, if you had faith."

"Faith in what? I'm a borderline case, I know. You tell me I was once treated for subversion. But I am what I am, and my faith stops short at the Department of Mortic Revenue. If I really thought you had the slightest chance I might support you, Koralin, but, frankly . . ." She shook her head disconsolately.

"They must have said the same kind of thing seven thousand years ago," said Koralin, smiling mystically. "May I stay here for a day—two days."

Aubretia took a deep breath, then made her decision. "I'm sorry, Koralin. It's a risk I dare not take. I'm convinced that security are watching me. It wouldn't be fair to you, or me, or to the child."

The disappointment that darkened Koralin's eyes was suppressed almost instantly. She looked down at the child, still lying white and motionless on the table, but there was no softening of the hard determined lines around her mouth.

"Aubretia, I appeal to you . . ."

"I'm sorry. I must ask you to go."

Koralin picked up the child. "We'll get by. Security is never one hundred per cent perfect, not in seven thousand years. Have you a car, Aubretia?"

Aubretia nodded.

"May I take it for a few days? I'll have it returned."

"They'll be stopping all cars."

"I'll take a chance. I may be able to cut across country in the outer suburbs."

Aubretia frowned "I wouldn't want the car damaged . . ."

"Aren't you prepared to make any kind of sacrifice?"

"For what? I can't believe in your dream, Koralin If they arrest you in my car then I'll be in trouble I don't want to be involved. All I ask is to be left in peace."

"All right. We'll leave you in peace "

Carefully Koralin wrapped up the inert child in the paper and placed it in the plastic bag, pushing the crimson cloak on top. Her movements were methodical and unhurried. When she had finished she took the bag by its handle and moved towards the door.

She turned finally towards Aubretia and said: "Give me one hour, please."

"One hour?"

"Before you call the police."

Aubretia seemed to sag a little, breathing deeply "Trust me, please, Koralin, in spite of whatever I did two years ago and whatever you think of me now; trust me this once. I shan't call the police."

"Thank you," said Koralin simply. Clutching the bag tightly she went through the door into the darkness of an unguessable future.

After Koralin had gone Aubretia went out on to the balcony overlooking the city. Her mind was tranquil enough, for she had already dismissed Koralin and her strange quest as an irrelevancy. The streets below, warmly floodlit, were peaceful enough, and the lights of the tall buildings were calm and colorful. There was nothing to indicate the tightening web of security, and indeed, security might have been a myth.

For the good citizen, she thought, *life is pleasant enough. Security is for the misfits, the agitators, the wild dreamers who might undermine the stability of the State. Women like Koralin, for instance, who not only pursue their own tortuous antisocial concepts, but seek to drag others into the engulfing whirlpool of their intrigues. As for the male child, it was nothing but a freak. The human species had progressed beyond the shallow condition of heterosexuality. The primitive and crude had been abandoned millennia ago, and human reproduction was now an exact science. Society was stable, the future secure, and the good citizen had nothing to worry about.*

Unless . . . another horrific thought stabbed needlelike at her brain. *Supposing they discovered that Koralin had been here, in her apartment, with the male child? They would inevitably interrogate her, check up on every movement since she had left the laboratory in Lon, and the truth would emerge. Aubretia, they would say, the woman with a record. Two years ago she underwent hypotic re-orientation for subversion, and now she has done it again. She has harbored a criminal without notifying security. And they would confer with the Department of Mortic Revenue and decide whether her potential usefulness in society was enough to justify continued survival, or whether this second lapse merited judicial euthanasia.*

Panic seized her heart with icy fingers. Trembling and chilled she hurried into the thermostatic warmth of the apartment and pressed the button on the videophone.

"Please," she said urgently, "get me security, quickly . . ."

Two days later Aubretia found a letter waiting for her on her return from the office. It was written in Valinia's tiny, neat handwriting and had been slipped under the door. Aubretia frowned as she picked it up, remembering that her friend from the apartment below had stayed away longer than usual on this latest visit to Lon.

She removed her cloak, sat down and read the letter.

Dear Aubry: When you receive this I shall have come and gone. I am returning only to pack, and then go back to Lon. My assignment here is finished. You never suspected, did you, Aubry, that I was planted on you for security purposes? But now you have nothing to fear. Your record is good, and after your exposure of the Koralin woman the other night, the Controller of Internal Security has decided that you no longer need supervision.

Unfortunately we have not yet located the Koralin woman or test four-six-five We believe she is still in Birm, but reports suggest that other women are now involved, and they may act as a chain to smuggle the specimen out of the country. If you hear anything, contact security immediately.

The trouble is spreading. Since experiments in micro-cytology have been stopped, cytologists throughout the world are protesting. Some are demanding that test four-six-five should be allowed to survive. It is amazing how quickly news travels. The poison seems to be creeping into some of the civil population, too, particularly in Asia, where the syn-

drome is probably weaker than elsewhere. Several attempts have been made to sabotage units of the world brain network, and other public utilities and government offices.

We are not anticipating such disorder in this country, but we have to be prepared. There is a full security mobilization, which is why I have been recalled to Lon. Apart from a general air of restlessness, especially among the scientific strata of society, there have been no demonstrations.

It is strange how a small thing can unbalance a perfectly planned society. Perhaps stability is geared in some way to purpose and direction, and perhaps the stabilizing factor was research into the synthetic creation of a male human. Without that focal point of endeavor, like the nucleus of a cell, it may be that society tends to lose its purpose, to disintegrate. The psychology of a social perversion-neurosis is very complex.

However, the situation is under control. When we have apprehended the Koralin woman and test four-six-five, we shall be able to enforce complete stability once more. Until then . . .

The explosion flung one of the windows of the room inwards in a cascade of glass splinters. The building shook as if in the steel grip of an earthquake. Alarmed, Aubretia dropped Valinia's letter to the floor and crossed cautiously to the window.

There was something wrong with the sky. Towards the east the deepening purple of approaching night was aflame with a livid, orange stain. An alarm bell sounded remotely, echoing from the walls of the buildings lining the cavernous streets. As she watched incandescence burst into spontaneous life further south, in the direction of the Department of Statistics. Another shuddering explosion occurred. More alarm bells, and in the road far below the distant murmur of excited voices grew.

She stared in horror at the glowing stains of destruction

in the sky. "It has started," she told herself fearfully. "Things are worse than Valinia said. All because of one male child. This is the end of all things . . ."

But a voice in the darkness of her mind whispered: "This is only the beginning . . ."

PUBLISHER'S POSTSCRIPT

While the manuscript of WORLD WITHOUT MEN was being prepared for publication, the staff of Ace Books were startled to see two news items, appearing independently, which unexpectedly underline the credibility of Charles Eric Maine's novel. One appeared in a story in the *New York Times,* for Oct. 16, 1957. This told of the announcement at a meeting of a "planned parenthood" society of advanced work on a "synthetic steroid tablet" to be taken orally to create a limited period of sterility. Several such projects are being experimented with in various laboratories, with a certain amount of success.

The other item is from the Nov. 9, 1957 issue of *Science News Letter,* the cover of which featured a photo of a healthy young turkey created by parthenogenesis without the aid of a male parent. The article spoke of new advances in the technique of producing "spontaneous embryos" in poultry by a method of vaccinating the females of the species.